BRIGHTON WALSH

COPYRIGHT

Edited by Lisa Hollett of Silently Correcting Your Grammar
Cover Design by Brighton Walsh
Cover Image: Clever by Wander Aguiar

Digital ISBN: 978-1-68518-013-3
Paperback ISBN: 978-1-68518-014-0
Special Edition Paperback ISBN: 978-1-68518-022-5

For all the girls who've been told they're too much
and who rock that shit anyway.

CHAPTER ONE

BRADY

BEING a small-town sheriff did not mean a cushy job with a lot of time off. It wasn't even 6:30 a.m., and I'd already answered a call for a suspected break-in that turned out to be a rogue raccoon, dealt with a domestic dispute, and changed a tire for an older lady stranded on the side of the highway. That last one was going to make me late if I didn't haul ass. And I refused to be late, especially when it came to family meetings with my siblings.

I pulled off the highway onto the road clearly marking Starlight Cove Resort and swept my gaze along the path, keeping my eyes peeled for anything unusual or out of place.

Like a 5'4" pain in my ass who just wouldn't leave.

Or do what she was told.

Or follow the laws so I could stop arresting her.

I'd lost count of how many times I'd cuffed Starlight

BRIGHTON WALSH

Cove's newest resident, Ms. Lancaster. Her latest infraction had been the day before when she'd thought it imperative to chain herself to a tree to stop the much-needed development of a piece of unused land that bordered my family's resort.

It must've been my lucky day, because I didn't see the infuriating woman as I drove down the path dotted with cottages. Though, it was still early. She probably didn't crawl out of her gremlin hole until at least eight, so I had a bit of a reprieve.

Outside the passenger's window, the waves of the Atlantic Ocean crashed against the rocky shore, the water glittering from the sun. I might've grown up here and spent every day of my childhood running down these gravel paths, the ocean's roar at my back, but I'd never tired of the view. Or of this place. It was home.

I glanced at my watch, noting I had only three minutes to spare, and relaxed my shoulders as I parked in front of the main inn that'd seen better days.

This whole place had seen better days.

The furnishings in the cottages were dated, the small front porches battered, and the siding could use a good painting at the very least. The whole place was in desperate need of a giant facelift. For an oceanfront resort, it didn't get nearly as much occupancy as it should, though that wasn't a surprise. Not after a couple of big-time house flippers had swooped in during a downturn in the market, bought up a bunch of tiny bungalows on the beach, refurbed them all to look the same, and then slapped them up on the nation's largest short-term rental site. Tourists flocked to them, which meant some out-of-state team was pulling in the money, not the small, locally run resort that had been in our family—and in this town—for three generations.

We'd been slashing prices and increasing amenities for two years, and nothing was helping. We were barely staying afloat, and it showed. This resort—our mom's dream—was dying a slow, painful death, and if I didn't figure something out, and soon, it'd take the whole family with it.

Something I refused to let happen.

I slid out of my patrol car and strode to the door, pulling it open to the sound of my family bickering, as per usual. I followed the noise past the front entry turned check-in counter and through the sitting room until I reached the once-pristine dining room. Now, the navy-and-white striped wallpaper was peeling in random spots, the white wainscoting needed a good painting, and the floors were scuffed and faded. Four out of five of my siblings sat around the oval table—what had once been our family dining table—their attention more on getting their morning fill of coffee than on the fact that I'd arrived just under the wire.

Even though the sun was barely up, Aiden, my Irish twin at eleven months younger than me, was already dressed in a crisp white button-up and tie, his navy suit jacket carefully folded over the back of his chair. Why he felt the need to dress up when the few guests who stayed with us roamed around in little more than swimwear, I had no idea. But since he was the face of the resort and ran this place day-to-day, I wasn't going to argue.

"So nice of you to join us," Beck grumbled. His brows were pinched as he stared at me from where he sat next to Ford—his actual twin. The antithesis of Aiden, Beck wore a plain tee, jeans, a backward baseball cap, and a scowl. "Some of us have a job to do."

I raised an eyebrow at him as I helped myself to some coffee, then pointedly glanced down at my uniform as I brought the mug up for a sip. I was technically on duty, but the weekly family meeting wasn't something I could get out of. Scratch that—it wasn't something I *wanted* to get out of. The only one who managed to do that was Levi, my youngest brother. He only bothered to show up once a month for budgeting—and even then, only when our baby sister dragged him there.

"I'm sure Everly will wait five minutes if you're not at the diner to open up exactly on time," I said behind my mug.

"That's not the point." He crossed his arms and narrowed his eyes. "Our posted hours say we open at seven."

Oh, I knew what the point was, and it had absolutely nothing to do with the posted hours and everything to do with the vivacious redhead who'd—beyond all reason—befriended Beck when she'd moved here two years ago.

"You bring any muffins, man?" Ford elbowed Beck and glanced around, as if his twin was hiding them under the table.

"We don't have the budget to feed your ass," Aiden said, pressing a finger to the stack of papers in front of him that detailed exactly how in the red we were.

"How about you idiots all shut the hell up so we can get started?" Addison, the youngest of our brood and only girl, said, her tone all business. For being such a little thing, she never showed fear or backed down from any of us. Though, she hadn't exactly had a choice, growing up with five older, overprotective brothers who weren't inclined to give her even an inch.

"How about you bite me?" Beck mumbled behind his coffee mug, but he turned to face her, just the same as the rest of us.

My four brothers and I may have been bigger, stronger, and older than she was, but nobody harbored a mean streak like Addison, and she had no qualms about unleashing it on us. In fact, she seemed to take great pleasure in it.

I settled into the seat next to Aiden and leaned back in the chair, taking a sip of coffee. It was black, just how I liked it, and utterly delicious. Beck ground this special blend himself, but hell if I'd let him know how much I loved it. He'd probably stop bringing it to meetings out of spite.

"Let's get on with it, then," I said, jerking a chin at Addison. "I can't stay here all morning."

Unlike the rest of you... But I left that part unsaid. They all worked at the resort—Aiden on main desk duty, Beck running the diner, and Addison running, well, everything else. Ford was our resort handyman in addition to his firefighter duties for the county. And Levi was the captain of the boat tours—when he bothered to give them. I was the only one who didn't rely on this resort for their livelihood.

And it ate at me every day.

I loved my job, loved the routine, the certainty of it, but not a day went by that I didn't wonder if everything would've been different now if I hadn't veered off onto this path. If I'd stuck close to home and stepped into the family business instead of venturing out on my own.

Would she still be gone?

Addison stared at me as she took a slow, deliberate sip out of her coffee mug, one eyebrow raised slightly as if daring me to say a word while she took her sweet-ass time. When my only response was a tick of my jaw, she finally cleared her throat. "I got an email from a travel magazine, *Weekend Wanderlust.* They're doing a spread on the best coastal resorts in the country, and they're sending someone to check us out to see if we'd be a good fit."

Interest piqued, I sat up, bracing my elbows on the

table, and leaned toward her, my brothers all mirroring my position. "Is that a popular magazine?"

"Second-largest circulation in the country."

"Holy shit," Ford muttered under his breath.

Addison nodded. "I don't need to tell you guys just how important this is for the resort. Getting selected to be included would be a huge write-up and would mean national publicity for the resort. Which means an influx of new guests, which means an influx of money." She pinned each of us with a stare. "Desperately needed money."

"Yeah, we get it," Ford said, folding his arms behind his head as he leaned his chair back on two legs. "We're broke. So you keep telling us."

"She keeps telling you because nothing's changed." Aiden shoved a few papers across the table toward the twins—the budget, no doubt. I didn't need to see it. I'd already caught a glimpse last night when I'd swung by to see him after my shift. Right before I'd transferred some money from my account to the resort's.

To say it wasn't good was an understatement.

"You've known me for thirty-two years, so I'm not sure why you think these numbers are going to mean anything to me." Ford passed the papers over to Beck without glancing at them. "You know I was more of a shop guy than algebra."

"Then let me put it in clear terms for you," Addison said. "We're—"

"Fucked," Beck finished for her, his eyes scanning the papers.

"Fucked," Addison confirmed with a nod. "If we don't figure out a way to get paying customers here, and fast, this resort is going to fold whether we want it to or not."

I glanced around at my siblings, each of their mouths set in a grim line. They knew as well as I did that we'd been running on fumes for far too long. This wasn't sustainable, but we didn't have a choice. Our whole lives were here, wrapped up in these nineteen cottages amid the winding road that followed the curving shore of the ocean. The ocean that had been our backyard our entire lives. They were in the walls of this home that we'd turned into the main inn nearly ten years ago.

"How long?" I asked, voicing the question everyone was wondering but unwilling to ask. How long did we have until we would have to call it quits?

Addison lifted a single shoulder. "Couple of months, if we're lucky. We're coming into tourist season, so that may save us a bit. But it's bad."

Aiden closed his eyes as he pinched the bridge of his nose. Ford ran a hand through his hair, dividing glances between Aiden, Addison, and me. And Beck...Beck just looked resigned.

I may not have worked at this resort, but it was as much mine as it was theirs. And none of them was in the right mind to take the reins, too close to see the forest for the trees. So I did what I did best and stepped up to take the lead.

"Tell us what you need from us," I said to Addison.

The corner of her mouth twitched—the only sign of her gratefulness—and she nodded. "Ford, I'll need your help working through a list. We don't have much of a budget, but—"

"Do what you need," I said. "I'll cover it."

She pursed her lips like she wanted to argue but must've thought better of it, because she continued with a short nod. "I'd like to get as much cosmetic work done as we can. We need to make this seem like a no-brainer. That Starlight Cove is the perfect, picturesque location with perfect, quaint residents. That it's basically a modern-day Mayberry set on the ocean, and this resort is the perfect getaway for some peace and quiet."

Ford crossed his arms and nodded. "That should be easy enough."

Addison snorted. "Normally, yes. But after Brady cuffed his friend yesterday, I'm not so sure."

"*My* friend?" I asked, incredulous. That insufferable woman wasn't anything remotely close to a friend. "Aren't you the one who kept telling me not to arrest her again?"

Ford glanced at me, brows raised. "Wait...who are you arresting? And what do you mean *again*?"

Addison waved a hand to dismiss his questions, her focus still on me. "I know you have some vendetta against Luna doing yoga on our property—"

"For the twelfth time, Addison, *she doesn't have a license*," I snapped. "And, as you've so eloquently put it, we're broke. If she's doing yoga on our property, she"—I held up my hand and counted off on my fingers—"one, needs a fucking license to do so, and two, should pay us for the use of the land, at the very least, considering we're broke."

"That's—" She cut herself off, her head tipping to the side. Before saying anything else, she pulled out her phone, her thumbs a blur on her screen as she mouthed whatever note she was writing herself. "That's actually not a bad idea..." she murmured.

"*What's* not a bad idea?" Beck snapped. "Jesus, woman, I'm going to cut off your morning coffee if you can't focus during these meetings."

"Don't threaten the person with the contacts to get you your beloved blackberry vanilla bourbon jam." She glared at Beck, who looked like he wanted to strangle her but finally settled back in his seat with nothing more than a grunt.

"As I was saying..." She raised her eyebrows at us, as if daring us to talk back. When none of us did, she continued, "Right now, I'm more worried about what's going on at the boundary of the resort. Luna's latest stunt is drawing negative attention."

"The development of the land," Aiden clarified, sorting through his stack of papers before he found what he was looking for and tossing it to the middle of the table.

The glossy, trifold brochure boasted a company called Holton Real Estate Group. Showcased on the front of the pamphlet was a variety of buildings they'd done, all big-box stores. Unlike the house flippers who'd swooped in, made their changes, and fucked over the town without so much as a peep, this company had held a meeting in town hall and informed everyone about their plans. From what they'd shown, this new store would bring more jobs into Starlight Cove—something we could definitely use—and provide a shopping experience we'd usually have to drive an hour-plus for. It would breathe some much-needed life back into the town, which would bring more revenue, which would be a good thing for all the residents and businesses, us included.

"More accurately, her protesting it," Aiden said. "Brady took her to the station yesterday for it, but she swore she'd be back."

I grunted in the affirmative. "The she-devil doesn't know when to quit."

"Okay, so what does this have to do with the resort and the article?" Ford asked, brows drawn.

"Any stink that's raised around town could be a sign to the magazine that Starlight Cove is too volatile of a destination to promote," Addison said. "Their whole vibe is rest and relaxation, and driving past a protester chained to a tree with sirens flashing just to get to the resort doesn't exactly scream peaceful."

"I hardly think that old bat Mabel and her Facebook

Lives will draw enough negative attention to warrant concern," Beck muttered dryly.

"Maybe not. But if this journalist shows up and catches wind of it, or if Luna refuses to back down without a fight, that could draw enough attention to be a detriment to us," Addison said.

I scrubbed a frustrated hand over my short beard and sighed. With all the work that needed to be done on the resort, the last thing any of them needed to worry about was this thorn of a woman who was hell-bent on making our lives as difficult as possible. "You guys just focus on getting the resort spruced up as quickly as possible. I'll handle Luna. Besides, maybe she'll surprise us and give up."

My radio crackled to life, and my deputy's voice rang out. "Sheriff, we've got a trespasser down at the old Williamson property. Reports claim she's chained herself to a tree. Again."

"Well, so much for that." Beck stood and slapped a hand on my shoulder. "But maybe swing by the diner on your way out. I'll send you with something to sweeten the deal since your approach can be a bit...brusque."

That was something, at least, because I didn't think Luna would be inclined to agree to help us after I'd read her her rights and tossed her, handcuffed, into the back of my patrol car for the second day in a row.

CHAPTER TWO

LUNA

WHEN I'D FIRST SET foot in Starlight Cove a month ago, I hadn't come here intending to chain myself to a tree. Obviously. But like my parents always taught me, I needed to take the opportunities life presented. So who was I to ignore it when information landed in my lap—like the times the soulless assholes arrived at this site in the morning, or just exactly when they planned to start tearing up this beautiful, untouched land? And if the hardware store in town just so happened to carry my preferred lock and chains, and I just so happened to be released from yesterday's...incident...with plenty of time to get over here? Well, I wasn't going to look a gift horse in the mouth.

Sitting cross-legged at the base of the mammoth tree that would be my companion for the second day in a row, I rested my palms on my knees and closed my eyes, centering myself. If I listened carefully, I could almost hear the crashing waves of the ocean like I'd grown accustomed to greeting me each morning from my converted van parked along the shore in the forest preserve.

In the time I'd been in this sleepy little town, I'd taken to completing my morning Vinyasa just across the boundary of the preserve, a short walk from where I was parked. I loved nature and I loved the trees, but I didn't want them blocking the view of my soul sister, the ocean. And yeah, *technically*, the boundary I crossed was the private property of Starlight Cove Resort, and *technically*, one of the owners of that resort was an ass with a penchant for arresting me, but the land was open and airy, much more so than the site I'd parked my van.

Who was I hurting anyway? I was just one petite woman. If people felt compelled to join me during my routine and then pay me for guiding them, well. What was I going to tell them? *No*?

Despite my less than pleasant reception from Starlight Cove's sheriff, I'd fallen in love with this place. It was a postage-stamp-sized pocket of paradise, right along the rocky Maine coast, a lush crown of forest to one side and a charming downtown only seen in movies to the other. I'd stumbled across it on my way home to Maryland for a quick visit, but I'd been so enamored of it and the people, I just...hadn't yet left. There was something so peaceful about it here. As soon as I'd arrived, it'd felt like my soul had settled. And, because I wasn't one to question the proclivities of my soul, I'd decided to stay put until the urge to leave cropped up again.

And it would. It always did.

Knowing I wouldn't have long until the cavalry arrived, I sank into a quick meditation. I breathed in deeply to a count of four, held for four, then released it in a slow, controlled exhale of eight. I liked to start my mornings as relaxed as possible, believing my beginning emotions held all the power to control my day. And I refused to let the intentions of the money-hungry corporation dead set on razing this land derail me.

I was calm. I was peaceful. I was—

"*You again,*" a male voice boomed from somewhere off to my left. "Just what in the hell do you think you're doing?"

The sound of quick footfalls echoed around me, warning me of his imminent arrival, but I didn't open my eyes. At least not until his shadow fell over me and I felt him looming above me.

I cracked open one eye and glanced up at the foreman I'd had the displeasure of meeting yesterday. He was in his late forties or early fifties, bald, with a beak nose and a protruding belly. He looked like my high school geometry teacher, Mr. Carson. I hadn't liked him much, either, though the worst he'd ever done was force me to find the volume of a trapezoid and not the deforestation of twenty acres of lush land inhabited by dozens of species of plants and animals.

"Morning." I smiled up at him, squinting into the sun peeking over his shoulder.

"'*Morning*'?" he repeated, his tone incredulous. Sweat dotted his forehead, though it was still cool outside, and he swiped his sleeve across it. Someone was getting a little stressed. Good, it served him right. "Like I told you yesterday, you can't be here."

I snorted, gesturing to the chains that bound me to the probably hundred-and-fifty-year-old tree at my back. "I assure you, I can, and I am. Obviously."

His face reddened even further—which, to be honest, I hadn't thought possible. "You need to unlock this *right now*," he spat, his voice rising with each word, spittle forming at the corners of his mouth. *Ew.* "We're on a tight schedule, and you're halting the progress!"

I shot him a wide smile. "Oh *darn*. I had no idea that would happen."

He ground his teeth so hard, I heard it from my perch on the ground. "Don't fool yourself, sweetheart. You're not doing anything noble here. People need this shopping center."

"Animals need their homes more, *sweetheart*."

Was there anything worse than a pompous man who talked down to you because you were a woman? Yes, apparently. A pompous man who talked down to you because you were a woman and who also happened to be in charge of demolishing twenty acres of wildlife.

"Animals don't pay the bills, lady. They're going to have to mooch elsewhere. And *you* need to leave. Now."

"No can do. I seemed to have misplaced the key. Whoops." I shrugged, giving him my best contrite smile, despite the fact that said key was safely nestled between my breasts, tucked into my bralette right next to the amethyst I'd placed there this morning.

"Fine," he said, pulling out his phone. "You've given me no choice but to call the sheriff again."

"Oh, good. Let me know when he gets here," I said, placing my palms back on my knees and closing my eyes. "We're on a first-name basis, you know."

The foreman didn't need to know the reason for that was because Sheriff McKenzie had arrested me more than once. He'd done it so many times, in fact, my rap sheet had nearly doubled since I'd been in this sleepy little town. I'd never met a man more controlled by the law—more controlled, period—than Brady. Never met one more gorgeous, either.

At the first arrest, I'd been annoyed. Then irritated. But after my fifth time in his cuffs, I'd started to find it downright amusing. If he wanted to waste his time running the paperwork on little old me, then who was I to deny him something that obviously brought him delight? Besides, it wasn't exactly a hardship to look at him.

Looming nearly a foot taller than me, he was gorgeous,

with his dark, tousled hair and pale-green eyes, close-cropped beard that couldn't hide his chiseled jawline, and a body that just wouldn't quit. He was *stacked*, with tree-trunk legs, biceps the size of my head, and an ass I wanted to sink my teeth into.

So yeah...as long as he kept his mouth shut, I had no problem getting up to some good trouble and enjoying the view when he showed up to ruin all my fun.

Brady

THE LAST THING I should've been doing was bringing food to the enemy, but Beck wouldn't drop it, insisting the *Luna Special* would work wonders in smoothing her ruffled feathers and cinch what we needed to happen—namely, keeping her away from trouble.

Still. I was the goddamn sheriff of Starlight Cove. I wasn't about to show up to a call with refreshments for the lawbreaker. At least, not unless she gave me no other choice.

I stepped out of my car, taking stock of the witnesses. Hopefully, this hadn't gotten out of hand already and word hadn't yet spread like it was wont to do in our little town.

"...coming to you live from the Williamsons' old place where, for the second day in a row, newcomer to Starlight Cove, Luna Lancaster, is taking a stand against corporate greed." A small, older woman sporting a hot-pink sweat-shirt and matching sweatpants, her gray hair still in curlers, stood off to the side, phone held out in front of her as she spoke.

I groaned, scrubbing a hand over my face as I changed directions and headed toward her. "Mabel. Can you not do this right now?"

She pinned me with a scowl, turning her phone on me. "Sheriff McKenzie. Are you saying the good people of Starlight Cove don't deserve to know what's going on in their fine town? I have an obligation to report the news, you know."

I snorted, using all my restraint not to shove the phone away from me. "I think you can relax. It's Facebook, not the Associated Press."

"True, but we've got one of those here, too." Mabel grinned, as if she was delighting in that fact and the shocked look on my face. "Showed up about five minutes before you."

I shot my gaze around until it landed on the only person out of place. Tall, blond, and statuesque, with an air that said she didn't belong here but was gracing you with her presence anyway. Harper Davidson. She'd spent summers at the resort in her teen years. She'd been insep-arable from Levi and his best friend back then, but I hadn't seen her here in years. "Harper? Since when do you work for the AP? I thought you wrote for some lifestyle magazine."

"I don't work for the AP," she said, coming to a stop next to us.

Mabel blew out a raspberry and swatted the air between them. "Oh, you're no fun."

Harper rolled her eyes. "But I *do* freelance for several lifestyle magazines who'd probably be really interested in the protestation of a new shopping development in Starlight Cove." She pursed her lips. "Too bad that angle won't be a good look for the feature about the resort..."

I froze, my eyes widening a fraction at that bomb she'd just dropped. Fuck. Of course, this couldn't have been easy. "You're writing the piece on the resort?"

"Sure am—*if* it gets approved." She pressed her lips together in some semblance of a smile, though it didn't quite reach her eyes.

That it was Harper behind this might actually work to our benefit. She'd spent so much time at the resort when she'd been younger, surely she'd want to feature it. Maybe I was the wrong McKenzie brother to talk to her, and Levi would have more luck. "Does Levi know you're here?"

Her stare hardened, smile dropping completely. "No idea. He's not exactly on my speed dial."

Well, shit. So much for that idea. I didn't know what had gone down between her and my brother, but it was clear there was no love lost between them. Not exactly a shock when it was Levi I was talking about. But their... entanglement definitely didn't bode well for securing a feature, which meant I needed to do everything to stack it in our favor.

"I'm working on taking care of this."

A raised brow was her only reply as I stepped around her and away from the incessant yammering of Mabel. I needed a clear head for what I was about to do. Luna and I had only spat fire and ice at each other since she'd first shown up in town. And if I didn't play my cards right, she could fuck up the one and only break the resort had had in years. I refused to let this woman prevent my family from getting what they needed.

Steeling my shoulders, I took a deep breath and prepared for battle.

Hands on my belt, I strode toward the too-beautiful-for-her-own-good woman who sat at the base of a huge tree, its trunk at least three times the width of her. She wore a pale gray sweatshirt and leggings that I knew first-hand would hug her shapely ass. Her dark hair was gathered off to the side in a thick, loose braid, with several smaller braids interspersed throughout and wisps of hair framing her face. It was infuriating, really, how gorgeous this pain in my ass was.

"Ms. Lancaster. Do you love handcuffs in general or just mine?"

A sparkle danced in her blue-hazel eyes as she looked up at me, her lips pursed. "Is that why you're here? You gonna arrest me again, Sheriff?"

"If I have to."

She jutted out her chin, her delicate features such a contrast to the firm set of her jaw. "Well, I've cleared my schedule, and I intend to be here all day, unless someone drags me away."

"Is that so?" I asked in a low murmur, then squatted down so I wasn't towering over her. "We just did this yesterday. Where's the key?"

She sniffed, looking far too poised for someone who was sitting in the dirt and chained to a tree. "Must've lost it."

"Mhmm." I didn't believe her for a second, especially since she'd given me the same line yesterday and then dug it out of some hidden pocket in her leggings. She was reckless, yes, but she wasn't stupid. She had that key tucked somewhere safe on her person. I just needed to find it. Preferably soon, before we gave Harper any more fodder for an article than she already had. "Last chance."

"You might as well do whatever you planned, because nothing will make me give up that key."

With a sigh, I stood. "I didn't want it to come to this."

Without another word, I turned and headed back toward my patrol car. I was trusting Beck with the small bit of intel he'd given me before I'd left the resort and headed over here. Apparently, my little lawbreaker ate breakfast every morning in the diner—some crazy, new-age vegetarian, gluten-free, soy-free, flavor-free concoction no sane person would put anywhere near their mouths—but she hadn't this morning. I was counting on her being hungry and caffeine-deprived for this next part to work.

"Are you getting a Taser?" Luna called after me, drawing the attention of not only nosy Mabel, but also a sharp-eyed Harper. "Or are you going for the pepper spray? Whatever it is, it doesn't matter. You'll need bolt cutters to get me away from this tree! I'm doing this for the animals who can't speak for themselves."

My God, could the woman be any more dramatic? Or infuriating? She set my teeth on edge, and I had to beat down the part of me that wanted to punish her for misbehaving. With my hand on her bare ass.

"Sheriff, can you let the good people of Starlight Cove know what's going on? Who chained Luna to the tree and just left her there to perish?"

"Mabel," I snapped, what little patience I had long gone. "*Go home.* You're not even reporting the facts. No one did this to her—she did it to herself."

Mabel pressed the phone against the material of her sweatshirt and shot me a wink. "Nothing wrong with spicing up those facts a bit. Embellishing and whatnot. Gets me more views and likes, and that's what it's all about."

I grunted in response but otherwise ignored her as I reached in and grabbed the bag holding a takeout container and the to-go cup full of the disgusting green concoction Beck had tricked me into trying. It tasted like weeds and ass, and if I never had it near my mouth again, it would be too soon.

Thankfully, Harper was quite a ways away, her back to me as she talked with the foreman while I carried my... bribe—I cringed at the thought—toward Luna. The last thing I needed was Harper writing this up in her article.

"Food delivery for the person breaking the law." Mabel tsked, eyebrows raised. "Trying a new tack, Sheriff?"

"Mabel, if you're not gone in two minutes, I'll arrest you for trespassing along with Ms. Lancaster."

She gasped and held a hand to her chest. "You *wouldn't*. What would your mother say?"

It was the same question I'd asked myself every day for nearly ten years. But in all that time, I'd gotten damn good at forcing it down and ignoring it, so I did it once again.

"Don't push me."

She narrowed her gaze on me, but she must've seen the steely glint in my eyes proving that I wasn't in the mood for her shenanigans today, because she turned away without another word and spat some nonsense into the phone I couldn't be bothered to pay attention to.

Not when I had one mission while I was here—remove Luna from the location and make her agree to stay out of trouble by whatever means necessary.

Images of a naked Luna, spread out and handcuffed to my bed, flashed through my mind, and I had to clench my teeth against them. My dick didn't seem to care that she was a royal pain in my ass and dead set on making my life a living hell. It only cared that she was soft and beautiful, feisty and wild, with the kind of curves a man wouldn't get sick of, even after a lifetime.

Fortunately, though, I hadn't been ruled by my dick since I was fourteen, and I had no intention of reverting to that now.

CHAPTER THREE

LUNA

BRADY'S polished black shoes stopped just in my line of sight, and I roved my gaze up the long, muscled lines of his body, not stopping until I met his sea-glass green eyes. Because the Universe apparently had a sick sense of humor, the man looked like a walking sex god, all broad shoulders and thick biceps, dark, messy hair, and a trimmed beard just long enough that I'd definitely fanta-sized about what it'd feel like against my inner thighs.

Too bad he was such a buzzkill. He was so rigid, so controlled, he probably couldn't even let loose during sex. I bet it was all missionary, lights off, straight to business. Going down on a woman was out of the question, no doubt. Far too messy.

Before I could ponder what else he wouldn't do in the bedroom, he squatted down in front of me and set a to-go cup I knew was from the diner on the ground next to him.

He pulled out a takeout container from the bag he carried and opened it. And then the bastard waved it under my nose, allowing the mouthwatering aroma to drift toward me.

"Did Beck make that food for me?" I asked, trying to contain the drool threatening to escape my mouth.

Since I'd arrived in Starlight Cove, I'd made it one of my missions to open the chef's eyes to all the varied possibilities of offering an expanded menu. A farm-to-table type thing with vegetarian options. Doing so would appeal to more diners. And, well, if the newer offerings were more sustainable and helped the local farmers and economy, all the better.

"Not sure I'd go so far as to call this food..." He looked at the breakfast in disgust.

I leaned forward as much as my chains would allow and peered into the container, and I couldn't stop my mouth from watering. Yep, just as I suspected. My favorite.

He was playing hardball, but I could too.

"I'll make you a deal, Sheriff. Give me the omelet, and you can have the drink." I tipped my chin toward what had to be my morning cocktail—green juice consisting of wheatgrass, kale, spinach, pineapple, cucumber, and ginger.

"I'm not sure what gives you the impression that you're in a position to bargain. Besides, I'd rather drink toilet water than whatever that shit is." Brady settled the to-go container on his knee, just out of my reach. "Doesn't matter anyway, because I'm keeping it all until you unchain yourself."

I narrowed my eyes on him. This slick son of a bitch knew exactly where to hit me so it'd hurt. He talked with his family daily, and Beck had probably let him know I hadn't been by that morning, so he was here to feed off my weaknesses—namely that I hadn't eaten since yesterday. I was strictly a three-to-four meal a day kind of person, and I'd already failed to get in first and second breakfast. Brady might be ruled by order, but I was ruled by my stomach, and he clearly knew that. Said stomach took that moment to let me know of its disapproval. Loudly.

Normally, I wasn't so easily swayed. It took a lot more than a bribe that made my mouth water to get me to walk away from something I believed in, but this day was already shaping up to be a dead end for the foreman, considering the forecast called for an eighty-five percent chance of rain, and I'd already felt the soft sprinkling of showers beginning. A rain-soaked ground would keep them from moving forward today. As for tomorrow... Well, I'd be right back here to do this all over again.

When I didn't respond, Brady just raised a single brow. I'd never seen this man look anything but two things—pissed off or irritated—but right then, if I didn't know better, I'd say he looked downright smug. How he managed all three while looking like a cover model for *Grumps Weekly*, I had no idea.

With a sigh, I reached into the front of my sweatshirt,

not missing the way his gaze fell to the low-cut scoop of my neckline, his eyes heating for a moment before darting away. "Fine. But this isn't over. You know I'll just be right back here tomorrow morning. And the day after that. And the day after that."

"What happened to your resolve?" a woman called from somewhere off to my left. "What about the animals? You're just giving up, and for what? Some eggs?"

Brady snapped his gaze in the direction of the voice, and I watched with poorly placed fascination as his jaw ticked, his thick fingers curling around the takeout container. What would it be like to have all that control unleashed?

While in bed.

Naked.

"What'd I tell you, Mabel?" he barked. His voice held a low warning that shot straight to places inside me it had no business going.

Shifting on the ground to relieve some of the misplaced excitement, I followed his gaze to where the sweet—if nosy—eccentric older lady stood, holding out her phone toward us.

Mabel shrugged, completely unrepentant. "My fans count on me to report the news, Sheriff. And we have—" she paused to look at the screen " —twelve people watching now. Gotta keep them informed."

That woman was the eye of the hurricane in this small town. Gossip seemed to swirl around her wherever she went—or she brought it with her, I wasn't quite sure. Last week, she'd placed a custom order for face cream from me, and when I'd dropped it off for her, she'd kept me there for forty minutes, spilling the latest tea—Randall was *totally* cheating on his poor wife, Dorothy, by the way. Regardless, she was amusing, and her Facebook Lives were legendary around these parts, especially since the newspaper didn't seem to delve too far into the nitty-gritty of Starlight Cove.

"These aren't just any eggs, Mabel," I called, wanting to make sure Beck got credit where credit was due. "It's an all-organic egg-white omelet with fresh goat cheese, heirloom tomatoes, and sprouts. Beck calls it the Luna Special."

"That's because you're the only one who'd eat this shit," Brady grumbled under his breath, his focus back on me. "You going to unlock that chain, or am I tossing your food to the animals you're so worried about?"

"Fine," I snapped, fumbling with the key as I attempted to fit it into the lock at this weird angle. "I'll do this but only because it's already raining and is supposed to continue all day, so they won't get far anyway."

"Whatever you need to tell yourself, lawbreaker."

"Are you sure you and Beck are related? He's so welcoming."

He snorted. "That's the last word I'd use to describe Beck."

"Fine, welcoming in a surly kind of way. At least he's not a complete curmudgeon like you."

Brady snapped his mouth shut as his face reddened.

He looked even more pissed than usual, and that was saying something. "You're awful mouthy for someone who's about to be handcuffed in the back of my car."

"Not my first time, Sheriff." I winked as I freed myself from the chains and stood, stretching my limbs over my head and dipping side to side before sinking into a standing forward bend. I'd only been there for a couple hours, but it'd been long enough to get stiff. "Do you have a fork for all that deliciousness?"

He didn't answer right away, so I stood upright and glanced at him over my shoulder, just in time to see his eyes dart away from wherever he'd been staring. My ass? No way...I had to be mistaken.

"In the car," he finally said, grabbing the to-go cup from the ground and standing to his full height where he towered over me. He had to be 6'3" at least, and the man was seriously sex on a stick, especially in his uniform. Why was it always the hot ones who were assholes?

"Thought you were gonna cuff me." I fell into step next to him, giving Mabel and the phone she directed our way a quick flutter of my fingers.

"Keep running your mouth, and I will."

"I didn't realize you could do things that were against the rules."

He glared down at me as he opened the back door to his police car. "So you *do* understand the concept of rules."

"Understand them?" I slipped into the now-familiar back seat and shrugged, holding out my hands for the deli-

31

ciousness he held. "Sure. I just view them more as suggestions than guidelines."

"I'm well aware." He handed me the container of food and my drink before shutting the door and sliding into the front seat. Through the opened plexiglass panel, he passed back a fork. "Any chance your plans are taking you out of Starlight Cove today?"

I tucked into my breakfast, humming and closing my eyes as the first delicious bite hit my tongue. When I reopened my eyes, I met Brady's gaze in the rearview mirror and shook my head. "With food like this? I don't think so." I wrapped my lips around the straw, taking a long pull of my morning cocktail. "You never answered me before. You sure you and Beck are brothers? Someone who makes something this delicious surely can't be related to someone who looks like they suck on lemons for fun."

Holding eye contact and without answering, Brady slid the plexiglass partition closed, effectively cutting off communication with me and leaving me back here to think about what I'd done.

While he probably thought it'd been too much, I knew it hadn't been nearly enough, even two days in a row. My mom would've been so disappointed if she knew I'd folded because I'd slipped up and protested without coming prepared. That was, like, the first rule she'd taught me. I usually had a prepacked bag with all my essentials, but I'd forgotten to replace everything after yesterday's protest.

Unfortunately, I might not be able to keep this from

her. Not since my lawyer father was the one I called to help me out whenever trouble like this found me. And it'd been finding me a lot since I arrived in Starlight Cove. Or rather, *Brady* had been finding me a lot. If I didn't know better, I'd say he actually enjoyed arresting me.

I glanced toward him, taking in the sharp line of his jaw, the stiff set of his shoulders. The way he gripped the steering wheel so tightly his knuckles were white. I'd never met a man more in control than he was. Never met one who followed the law to the letter as much as he did.

Never met one I loved to torment quite as much, either.

CHAPTER FOUR

BRADY

WHY THE HELL did that woman get to me so damn much? She was like an itch I couldn't scratch. Or like a persistent fly that wouldn't leave me the hell alone, buzzing around all day but just out of reach.

I glanced over at her in the holding cell, her head tipped back against the wall and exposing her long neck, eyes closed, a soft smile on those plush pink lips, and I had to force myself to look away.

But it didn't matter.

Somewhere along the way during the time she'd been here—here, in Starlight Cove, yes, but also here, in the station—I'd looked at her enough that her features were seared into my brain. I could recall the exact twinkle in her eye when she said something she knew would piss me off. Knew the exact shade of copper streaked through her chestnut hair when the sun hit it. Knew the exact curve her lips tipped up into when she thought I wasn't looking.

Knew how goddamn hard she made me by simply breathing—not to mention having her curves on display while being forced to witness her flexibility. Nothing like having her ass directly in my line of sight to make my cock thicken enough that I'd worried it'd actually escape my uniform pants.

Fuck me, this woman was trouble with a capital T.

My desk phone rang before I could make my way to Luna, and I sank into my chair with a sigh. "Sheriff McKenzie," I answered.

"Sheriff, it's Mayor Drummond."

"Mayor." I relaxed back into my chair. "What can I do for you?"

"Seems there was another...scuffle out at the Williamsons' old place."

I blew out a heavy sigh. "How'd you hear about that?"

"It's spreading like wildfire. Mabel's Live already has four hundred views."

I couldn't hold in my gruff sound of irritation. Those goddamn Lives were going to be the death of me. "I've got it under control."

She hummed. "I'm not so sure you do. This is the second day in a row she's been there. Plus, don't you think perhaps you're sending a conflicting message to criminals when you show up with food and use that as a negotiation strategy?"

I liked the mayor—she'd been a close friend of my mom's and had been a part of my family my entire life—but there was a reason she was in public relations and not law enforcement.

"I did what I had to do to get her to leave as quickly and quietly as possible. I'm assuming that's what your call is about."

"Yes, that's the key here. Quickly and quietly. We don't want to cause a fuss for the developers."

I hummed—that was something we agreed on. "I assume you've already talked to Holton Group?"

"I have."

"And how do they want to proceed?"

"They're not happy she keeps showing up and halting progress, but they don't want the headache that pressing charges will bring. They let yesterday's infraction go with a warning, but she needs to pay a fine this time. And if she continues to show up, they'll have no choice but to press charges."

I grunted in agreement, my gaze darting over to Luna to find hers already locked on me. "I'll talk to her," I murmured into the phone.

"See that you do. And, Sheriff? Get her to see reason, will you?"

I barely held in my snort. I may not have known much about Luna Lancaster, but I knew, without a doubt, reason didn't even enter her realm of reality.

After hanging up, I strolled over to my little lawbreaker,

using my keys to unlock the holding cell, and tipped my head for her to follow me. "Let's go, Ms. Lancaster. We have a lot to discuss."

She swept out of the cell, far too close for my liking, her jasmine and lavender scent sweeping over me. Giving a goddamn Pavlovian response, my cock twitched in my pants, and I had to grit my teeth to keep myself in control. I hated that she had this effect on me. Hated that she tested my limits when I'd never, ever had that problem before.

She strode straight to the interrogation room, having done this far too many times, and I shut the door behind us.

She sat in the chair and folded her hands on top of the table. "I have nothing to say."

"Good. Because I have a lot to say, and it'll be a hell of a lot easier if you keep your pretty little mouth shut."

Her eyebrows rose, but I had no idea why. It wasn't the first time I'd told her to shut up. If she actually did, though, now *that* would be a first.

I sat down across from her, leaning back in my chair and crossing my arms over my chest. "Why do you feel the need to keep doing this shit? Did you not get enough attention as a child?"

She rolled her eyes. "When I was a child, my parents encouraged me to follow my passions."

"How lucky for me that one of your passions seems to be irritating the shit out of me."

Her lips curved up at the corners, and her eyes

sparkled with amusement. "That does seem to be a bonus, yes, but my protests have nothing to do with you, believe it or not. We should all care about the environment, Sheriff. If we don't put a stop to greedy corporations razing two-hundred-year-old trees just so we can buy lettuce and socks in the same store, there's not going to be any wildlife left, and then what will we have?"

"You're being a bit dramatic, don't you think? This is one tiny pocket of land—"

"One tiny pocket of land that happens to be a special value habitat which houses seventeen species of mammals, twenty-six different birds, and an immeasurable number of plants. Not to mention this pocket removes fifty-two tons of carbon dioxide each year."

I lifted my brows in surprise. I'd, apparently falsely, assumed she'd been doing this because she was bored. Not because she'd actually researched the possible ramifications and cared about them.

Regardless, it didn't matter. Having a new shopping center in Starlight Cove was going to be good for the community. I'd seen the plans and the proposal. On paper, it was exactly what we needed—something that would bring jobs and retain residents.

"That may be so, but this shopping center will only improve the town," I said. "That outweighs any possible ramifications you've found."

She shook her head, shooting me a look that could only be described as disappointed. "I shouldn't be surprised you wouldn't get it. Not everything is about money."

Only a spoiled princess who could travel the country in a converted van without worrying about pesky things like a steady job would say something like that.

"It's pretty apparent we're not going to agree on this," I said. "Though that's not exactly a surprise."

"Yeah, yeah, get on with the arrest already. The sooner you do, the sooner I'll be gone and can get back there to protest again."

I blew out a heavy sigh and sat forward, mirroring her position as I rested my forearms on the table. "That's where the problem is. If you show up back there again, Holton Group is going to press charges."

She snorted and rolled her eyes. "Sheriff, what about me makes you think I'm scared about someone pressing charges?" She leaned forward and met my gaze. "I don't care. The whole point is to make sure they can't move forward with the development. Whether or not I continue to be arrested is irrelevant."

There was no reasoning with someone like Luna. Someone with their head in the clouds and no grasp on the real issues facing people down on their luck. Which meant I needed to flip to Plan B and negotiate. My family just needed her to lay low for a couple weeks. Then she could protest all she wanted for all I cared, and I'd be right there to keep arresting her. It wasn't as if she'd be able to stop the corporation that'd set their sights on this land.

"What's it going to take for you to stop going back there?"

"Death," she answered with so much gravity, something hot and uncomfortable bubbled in my gut.

I ignored the foreign feeling and rolled my eyes. "Quit being dramatic, and let's see about a deal."

She raised a brow, clearly not having expected that. "That doesn't sound very sheriff-like. Did you manage to get that stick pulled out from your ass when I wasn't looking?"

"Spending a lot of time looking at my ass, are you, lawbreaker?"

She lifted a single shoulder. "I can admire a nice one when I see it. Doesn't mean I have to like the human it's attached to."

I brushed off her words that were undoubtedly intended to goad me and instead focused on what needed to be done. Namely, making sure Luna didn't screw up this opportunity for my family or this town.

"You need to lay off the protesting for the next couple weeks."

She huffed out a laugh. "Weeks? Not gonna happen. In that time, they could have the whole thing cleared."

"Doubtful. The forecast calls for storms the rest of this week."

"That only buys me a little time, and it's tumultuous at best." With her hands folded on the table, she leaned toward me. "If you want me to lay off, then I want you to fast-track the motion for discovery paperwork I submitted yesterday."

That paperwork was pointless and a waste of my resources, but if it'd get her to agree to this, then I'd do it. It wasn't like they'd find anything anyway. It'd only halt the progress for a short time, but a short time was all we needed.

"Fine. I'll handle it." But I sure as hell wasn't going to spare a lot of manpower for it. I'd send out one of my deputies with Mark, the high school biology teacher. Otherwise, we'd be waiting around for who knew how long to get someone down here, and Luna wouldn't be satisfied with that, which would only mean trouble. "But that's not all I need from you."

She pursed her lips and hummed low in her throat, the sound sending a shock wave straight to my cock. "Getting awfully greedy, aren't you?"

I clenched my jaw, forcing back all the unwelcome images that bombarded me featuring all the ways I could be greedy with her. Now wasn't the time or the place, and she sure as hell wasn't the woman.

"Can you be serious for two goddamn minutes?" I snapped.

She held up her hands in surrender, but the corners of her lips tipped up as if she was enjoying this back-and-forth. "Fine, fine. What else?"

"Harper, the journalist who was at the site this morning, is here doing recon for an article on getaways along the coast. If the resort gets featured, it would mean an influx of bookings, which would be good for everyone, the town included."

"Uh-huh..." she said, unmoved. "And let me guess—a protester going up against an evil corporation isn't exactly the wholesome, small-town vibe they're going for."

"Basically," I confirmed with a nod. "Look. I know you're new around here, but you genuinely seem to care about this town. That resort has been a part of Starlight Cove for over a hundred years. It was—" I stopped myself, clearing my throat as I broke off. She didn't need to know it'd been my mom's dream. That she'd loved it with her whole heart, which was why *we* loved it and why my siblings and I fought tooth and nail to keep it afloat. Luna just needed the barest of facts. "It just matters, okay? And if I have the ability to help it succeed, I'm going to do everything in my power to make it so."

Even if that meant getting creative with keeping Luna busy and out of the way.

She narrowed her eyes at me, studying me for long moments, before she nodded once. "Okay."

My brows flew up my forehead. I hadn't expected her to agree so quickly. "Okay?"

"I'll behave under a couple conditions." That was more in line with what I'd been waiting for.

"Who said you get to make any demands? Or did you forget you're the one in lockup?"

"You haven't arrested me. No Miranda rights." She

waved a hand through the air. "We're negotiating, so that's how this works. If you want me to behave, I want permission to lead yoga classes on the resort's property. I'm tired of being arrested every time I find my Zen. I'd much rather be arrested for actual important causes."

I narrowed my eyes, wondering if it could really be that easy. Especially since Addison had just been muttering about something similar this morning. "That...sounds reasonable."

"I'm not done."

I exhaled a long-suffering sigh. "Of course you're not."

"You also have to agree to attend two of those classes—as a willing participant—and receive one massage. My treat. You're looking a little stiff, Sheriff. Holding in all that stress isn't good for your body or your soul. As you've so generously proven."

I swept my gaze over her, from her mass of chestnut waves swept over her shoulder in a messy braid, to her blue eyes lit with a ring of fire around her pupil, to her full, lush lips lifted at the corners, to the delicate lines of her throat that I so desperately wanted to wrap my hand around while I—

I shook my head to clear those thoughts and tried to get a read on her. There had to be a trick in there somewhere, but I couldn't see it. Though, truth be told, being in her presence for the scant three hours she was demanding was going to be punishment enough. But if it'd help my family and the resort, as well as the town, I'd do it without question.

"Those are your terms? Fine."

"That's not all."

I leveled her with a stare that had made fully grown men wither in their seats. She just regarded me with amusement dancing in her eyes.

"I think that's plenty," I bit out.

She shook her head and crossed her arms over her chest. "One last thing or there's no deal."

"What is it?"

"A kiss."

I froze for half a second, sure I'd heard her wrong. "A...what?"

"A kiss," she repeated, not even a hint of a waver in her voice.

"From Beck?" The words tasted like acid on my tongue, though I had no idea why. It wasn't my business who she went around kissing, even if the other party was one of my brothers.

She snorted and shook her head. "From you. For educational purposes, of course. I want to see if you kiss like you do everything else."

"And how's that?"

"Utterly controlled and like you have a stick lodged so far up your ass, your tongue gets splinters."

I clenched my jaw, the urge to storm out of here pitted against the need to bend her over the table and smack her ass until my hand was imprinted on it. And then find other ways to occupy her mouth so she couldn't run it just to piss me off.

Not thinking about it a second longer, I stood and stalked over to her, pulled her straight out of her chair, sank my fingers into that lush mass of hair, and slammed my lips down onto hers.

With the amount of aggression that had built up between us in the time she'd been in town, it was no surprise that sparks erupted as soon as our mouths met. But that had nothing on the jolt of electricity that zipped through me and pooled in my cock when she parted her lips and our tongues slid against each other. I gripped her hair tighter as she moaned into my mouth. With her hands resting on my chest, she melted against me, her fists bunching the fabric of my uniform shirt. And I didn't even care that she was wrinkling it.

Couldn't be bothered by it.

Not when I already had to use every ounce of my restraint so I wouldn't reach down and grip her ass, slam her into a wall, and show her just how much she affected me. I was hard as fucking stone, and it was all because of her. All *for* her.

Christ, this woman. She was infuriating and intoxicating at once, and I had no business being sucked into her orbit.

But as we finally pulled apart, gasping, her eyes glazed and lips swollen from my kiss, I knew that would never be possible. As long as Luna stayed in Starlight Cove, I was totally and completely fucked. And not only had I just agreed to willingly subject myself to her presence, but I'd promised my family that I'd stay on top of her to make sure she didn't throw any more wrenches into our plans.

That meant I needed to ignore this blatant chemistry between us. Sweep it under the rug, go back to business as usual, and pretend like Luna Lancaster hadn't just shifted my entire foundation with one tiny kiss.

CHAPTER FIVE

LUNA

WELL, I certainly hadn't seen that coming. When I'd goaded Brady into kissing me, I'd assumed it would be stiff, dry, forced. Utterly and completely controlled, just like the rest of him.

Instead, I got heat and intensity and toe-curling passion I could still feel coursing through my body. My panties were ruined, for sure. And my outlook on Brady? Well. That might be ruined, too. If not completely demolished, then most definitely tainted.

What kind of man had that kind of passion buried underneath such a rigid facade?

"I already called Addison to let her know our...arrangement," he said, his voice low and gravelly from where he sat in the driver's seat as he drove us toward the resort.

Had he told her about the kiss, too? No, he wouldn't. He may have let me glimpse a crack in his armor, but I was certain it wasn't something he did often. I was also sure he wouldn't want anyone else knowing it had happened in the first place.

I didn't know whether I loved or hated that—after all, having a secret that only the two of us knew was more intimate than he probably realized. It certainly felt that way, with the electricity still arcing between us, even from my spot in the back seat—because God forbid, he allow me to sit in the front with him. But that was fine by me. I could study him better from this position. The man was tense. More so than usual. It was clear from the steel pipe I'd felt lodged against my stomach earlier that he'd enjoyed our connection. Maybe he was still feeling the effects of that...situation.

"Great." I leaned forward as far as I could, putting my face right up to the opening in the plexiglass partition. "When can I expect you in your first class?"

He grunted, and I bit back a smile. This was going to be fun as hell, no doubt. And my requirements had really only been because I enjoyed fucking with him. My main concern and the only reason I compromised my position was getting the motion of discovery through and doing so quickly. Even if they didn't find anything—which I'd bet my van wasn't going to happen—Holton Group would have to halt all progress until the discovery was complete.

"With your track record, I'm going to make sure you don't show up at the site tomorrow before I fill my end of the bargain." He rolled to a stop in front of the diner and slid out of the car before opening my door.

Uncaring of the light rain, I stepped out, his tall, muscled body mere inches from me. Unable to stop myself from touching him, I crawled my fingers up his chest until I lightly patted his cheek, his short beard tickling my palm. "I always keep my word, Sheriff. And I expect you to do the same."

His jaw clenched like he had more to say but decided to force it down, and he jerked his head toward the diner. "Addison's in there."

"Perfect. I need to thank Beck for my delicious breakfast anyway."

With that, I strode away from him and toward the diner, loving the feel of the light rain on my skin. And if I threw a little extra sway into my hips just for Brady, well, who was going to call me on it?

"I'll let you know when my first class will be. Hopefully you can find some spandex between now and then." I tossed a grin at him over my shoulder before I opened the diner door.

He stared after me, his jaw clenching, and his expression...angry? Well, that wasn't anything new, but I'd sort of hoped we'd come to a cease-fire after the kiss that rocked the world. Apparently not.

"So, I hear you're our new employee," Addison said by way of greeting. She stood behind the counter, hands propped on her hips, eyes narrowed on me.

While I hadn't been expecting flowers and a celebration party, this still threw me a bit. Of all the McKenzies, she was the friendliest—barring Ford and his perpetual, almost automatic, flirtation.

"Um...yeah. That okay?" I asked as I sidled up to the counter and took a seat at the bar.

"Ignore her," Beck mumbled, filling a mug with coffee before sliding it my way. "She's just cranky because Mabel's Live about your protest had more views than her last tour of the resort."

I cringed, shooting her an apologetic look. I truly didn't want to cause this family any harm, because they'd been nothing but nice to me since I'd arrived. Okay, so that wasn't *entirely* true. I'd never actually met the elusive Levi, and Aiden was civil at best. And Brady? Well. Our interactions were definitely explosive. But Addison had greeted me warmly, even trying to convince Brady to stop arresting me in my early days here. Ford always kept me company, flirting in a way that proved he did so with everyone. And Beck fed me delicious food, even if he did so with little more than grunts.

"Sorry about that," I said, gratefully accepting the coffee. "I did give the diner a plug on the Live, though. Told them all about how amazing the Luna Special was."

Beck's mouth twitched, but that was as close to a smile as he gave.

"Still would've preferred you did that without chaining yourself to a tree," Addison grumbled, rolling her eyes. "It's not a good look for the resort being so close to that."

"So long as Brady fills his end of the bargain, I won't be back there..." I paused, quieting my next words as I hid my mouth behind my mug. "This week, at least."

"Speaking of," Addison said. "Brady filled me in, and I'll be real with you. We can't pay you anything. We're barely getting by as it is. But you can use the resort however you'd like and keep whatever you charge for the classes."

I waved her off, not concerned about it, having not even expected that much. When I'd sold my house back in Maryland and bought the van, deciding to travel instead of being locked to one location, shackled to one job, I'd garnered quite a nest egg. I'd barely had to dip into it, considering my living expenses were fairly minuscule on the road. And what few I'd had were covered by freelance gigs.

"I'm not worried about it," I said. "I just used it as part of the bargain to get your brother to stop arresting me."

Addison smirked, her eyes alight with mischief. "Yeah...I'm not sure this will stop him."

"It better. He promised." Although I couldn't deny the small part of me that would miss riling him up. He made my life difficult, without question, but there was no denying how utterly hot he was when he was all down-turned lips and fierce, furrowed brow...especially when all that ire and frustration were directed solely at me.

"Was this seriously all you wanted in exchange for backing down for a while?" she asked.

"What, teaching yoga?" At her nod, I hummed, a smile sweeping over my mouth. "No, actually. I wanted some paperwork fast-tracked. That was all I wanted, really, but why stop there when it's so fun to mess with him?"

Addison laughed, a bright, bold sound coming out of someone so tiny. "Oh God, what'd you do?"

I mirrored her grin. "He may also have to take two of my classes and get a massage. If he's still uptight after I've had my hands on him, he's beyond help."

Beck sputtered and choked on his coffee, hacking even as he waved Addison and me off when we regarded him with concern.

"You gonna live?" she asked her brother.

"Fine, fine," he sputtered out between coughs, his eyes watering as he avoided looking at us entirely.

"Come on," she said to me, stepping around the counter and tipping her head toward the door. "Let's get the paperwork filled out so Brady doesn't arrest me next."

Under her umbrella, we walked down the path toward the main inn, the sounds of the ocean lapping at the shore immediately setting my body at ease. The resort was slow, as it had been since I'd first arrived, and I couldn't ignore the pull in my stomach at my unease over the future of this place.

"This article is a big deal, huh?" I asked softly.

Addison shot me a look out of the corner of her eye,

her lips pursed as if she was debating how much to tell me. Finally, she said, "Yeah. Without it, I'm not sure—" She cut herself off and shook her head, pulling open the main inn's front door and closing the umbrella. "Well, I'm just not sure."

I followed behind her, stepping inside as the familiar warmth rushed over me. There was something so peaceful about this home, about this resort. Even though it was a little worse for wear, there was no doubt it was loved. That showed in the gorgeous flowers that lined the paths and bookended each cottage's porch steps. It was in the tray of baked goods that sat at the check-in counter, refreshed daily, and the snack baskets that peppered the communal areas of the inn.

This place deserved to prosper, and I hoped the motion of discovery took long enough that I wouldn't have to choose between helping this small-town business and the family I'd grown to care for or the acres of wildlife that no one else spoke up for.

Aiden stood behind the check-in counter, his crisp white shirt unbuttoned at the collar and his sleeves rolled up to reveal thick forearms. His jaw was dusted with a couple days of growth—not quite as thick as Brady's, but there was no denying the resemblance between the brothers.

His light eyes met mine, his brow turned down in a scowl. Normally, a look like that from his brother would shoot a flurry of excitement through me as I contemplated all the different ways I could torture him. That didn't happen with Aiden. Yes, the man was attractive. No one would be able to deny that. But he had nowhere near the pull on me that his infuriating brother did.

"Once we get you set up, you won't need to worry about pesky things like business licenses while you're here," Addison said, slipping around the back of the counter and pulling out a stack of paperwork.

It was something I obviously hadn't been worried about, but I shrugged all the same. "Sounds perfect to me."

"Wait...you do have a massage therapist license, right? And a certification for yoga?"

I grinned. "Yes, of course. I'm not *that* much of a rule-breaker. I take my obligations to people's well-being very seriously."

"Good." Addison passed over the papers, then held out a pen to me.

Before I could grab it, Aiden snatched it out of his sister's grasp. "Not so fast. I need a little more reassurance before I'll process this."

"What kind of reassurance?"

"You have to swear you won't protest again. At least until this article is secure."

The thought of not protecting what was important to me unsettled something deep inside. If I wasn't out there, I knew no one else would be, either, and that didn't sit right with me. "How long will that be?"

Aiden shrugged. "Couple of weeks?"

A couple of weeks with nothing standing in Holton Group's way could mean the land was cleared and the shopping center's foundation already poured. And that wasn't something I was willing to gamble on. But I didn't need to show my cards this soon, especially when nothing was set in stone. Brady had assured me he would fast-track the paperwork, and I knew enough that once that had been accepted, no further movement could happen until the discovery was complete. And anything before that? Well, I just had to hope the meterologist was right and storms were on the horizon.

"Deal."

Aiden narrowed his eyes on me, studying me for long moments. I didn't break his gaze, simply held out my hand for the pen. When he finally handed it over, I offered him a smile and set out to fill in the paperwork.

"I hope you're not going to need any special equipment for this, because we don't have the budget for it," Addison said.

I waved her off, keeping my eyes focused on the paperwork. "I've got what I need. I usually ask people to bring their own mats with them, but I have a few extras for those who don't have their own or just want to try it out. And I've got a portable table for any massages."

"Perfect. Now we just need to figure out a location. What kind of space do you need?"

"I'd like to do it outside whenever possible, and that little alcove I was using between Cottages Eight and Nine would be perfect. But do you have anywhere in here that would work for days like today when it's raining?"

Addison hummed and pursed her lips as she tapped a finger against them. "Probably the parlor would work best. There's not a lot of furniture in there, so it would be easy to clear out for a class."

"Is that the room with the wall of windows?"

"That's the one."

As if the room weren't gorgeous enough, with floor-to-ceiling bookshelves and a few cozy-looking chairs to curl up in, it also looked out over the most beautiful view of the ocean.

"Perfect." I shot her a smile, and she grinned back.

I'd still have to figure out something for the massage I'd cornered Brady into accepting, but that was a single session. If it had been in my plans to stay longer, I might have needed to worry about a permanent location for massages. But at this point, I had no intention of sticking around much longer than making sure Holton Group didn't get their claws into a piece of Starlight Cove.

CHAPTER SIX

BRADY

I DIDN'T NEED to look outside to know it was a full moon. It had to be, based on the clusterfuck that had been my day. There was the complaint about someone stealing three chickens from the Wilsons' farm, a drunk man roaming down Main Street wearing only a T-shirt, bare ass and all his dangly parts hanging out for the world to see, and a welfare check on a woman who called dispatch, high as a kite, and claimed the wolves were after her. Not to mention how it'd started by dealing with the pain in my ass known as Luna. Or that kiss...and my reaction to it.

If anyone pressed me on it, I'd say it was fine. Perfunctory. Uninspired and bland. I sure as hell wouldn't admit to it being the hottest kiss I'd had in recent—or even distant—memory and that I'd been hard enough to pound nails by the time I'd finally torn my mouth away from hers.

Christ, even the remembrance of her taste had me

groaning, my cock twitching in my pants, and I forced away thoughts of where else she'd taste just as sweet. I did not need to be thinking about Luna in any capacity, but especially not what it'd be like to have her naked and writhing beneath me. What I needed was to forget today had ever happened.

Intent on doing just that, I removed my gear, stowed my gun in my safe, and slipped into a T-shirt and sweatpants before heading downstairs to preheat the oven for my gourmet meal of frozen pizza. I could've gone to the diner and had Beck whip me up something to take home, but doing that would've meant interacting with my family, and given where my lips had been hours prior, I didn't think that was a great idea.

Before I could grab a beer and settle into my couch, my phone rang with Aiden's ringtone. For half a second, I contemplated not answering. I had little doubt as to what this call was about, considering just that afternoon, Luna had filled out paperwork to officially become an employee of the resort—one we definitely shouldn't have hired and almost certainly couldn't pay. Was it too much to ask to get a little reprieve from that insufferable woman?

Yes, apparently, because I knew if I didn't answer, one of two things would happen—he'd either call back, continually, until I *did* pick up, or he'd stop by and use his key to help himself inside.

Deciding a phone call was the lesser of two evils, I hit accept before it could go to voice mail. "Yeah."

"You're supposed to be keeping Luna in line, not having a goddamn spa day with her."

I pulled a beer out of the fridge and popped the cap before taking a swig. "What the hell are you talking about?"

"She told Addison you're taking two of her yoga classes *and* she's giving you a massage." Papers shifted on his end, probably from the front desk he couldn't drag himself away from, despite it being damn near seven o'clock. "So, what, you're consorting with the enemy now?"

I sighed, pinching the bridge of my nose as I dropped onto my couch, resting my beer bottle on my knee. I knew I shouldn't have answered. "I thought you liked her."

Every one of my brothers seemed to like her—with the exception of Levi, who, as far as I knew, hadn't met her— Beck especially, and I refused to pay attention to how much that rankled me.

"I like her fine," he said, his voice flat, as if he were discussing the new cashier at the Handy Mart. "I do *not* like how her latest whim could jeopardize the resort and the one break that's finally in reach."

My heart seized at the undercurrent of fear lacing Aiden's words. He was the levelheaded one of our group. The one who kept things on track. Who didn't get worked up if there wasn't a reason to. But he sure as hell was worked up now.

"It's going to be fine," I said, the bite gone from my

tone. "Luna and I..." I blew out a long breath and scrubbed a hand down my face. "We worked out an arrangement."

An arrangement where she tricked me into getting her lips on mine and making my whole goddamn world implode, but considering Aiden's current mind-set, it was probably best to keep that detail to myself.

"What happened to 'We don't negotiate with terrorists'?" he asked.

I rolled my eyes, settling back into my couch and taking a pull of my beer. "That's the federal government. They have way more resources than I do. I make do with what I have, and what I have is a couple deputies and Beck's cooking."

"And your time, apparently," he said dryly.

Not to mention my sanity. "Apparently."

Aiden grunted, his ire cooling dramatically. "At least she plugged the diner on the Live. That was...amiable."

Amiable wasn't exactly a word I'd use in reference to Luna. Infuriating, insufferable, recalcitrant...yes. Amiable? Not around me.

"Speaking of amiable," I said, "how long do I have to keep her...occupied?"

I had absolutely no excuse for why my brain supplied a litany of options I could enlist to keep her *occupied*, many of which involved my handcuffs but none of which involved talking. Or clothes.

"Probably a week." He paused. "Starting next week."

"Why the hell didn't you just say two weeks?"

"Because I figured you'd get pissy about that. I was right, by the way."

I bit back a growl of frustration. "I don't think you understand what you're asking of me."

Being around Luna tested my patience, my resolve, and my control more than anyone had ever done before. And I fucking hated it. Control was what had gotten me where I was today. It was what had kept this family running when everything else was crumbling down around it. Control kept me sane.

And Luna was like freeing a swarm of bees in the middle of Main Street or setting a zoo's worth of animals loose on the interstate—pure, unsuppressed chaos.

The smart thing to do would be to stay as far away from her as possible. Wait out the storm until she decided she'd had enough of Starlight Cove and took her tiny little tin can house and left in a haze of incense and essential oils, never to be seen or heard from again.

My stomach cramped as the thoughts flitted through my mind. Fuck, I needed to eat.

"Come on, it's not that bad," he said. "It's just until the journalist can get the lay of the land and see if the resort would be a viable option. And I fucking hope they see it as a viable option."

"Did you know the journalist scouting the place is Harper?"

"Harper?" he asked. "As in...Levi's Harper?"

"Don't think she's been Levi's anything for years, but

yeah. She didn't look real happy to be here, or to hear his name."

"*Fuck*," he groaned, drawing out the word, and I could nearly see him scrubbing a hand over his face. "We need this, Brady. I...I don't know if we'll survive without it."

Hearing Aiden admit what I already feared felt like a vise gripping my heart. This resort was the last thing we had of our mom—the one parent we'd always been able to count on, no matter that the other wasn't far. It'd been in her family for generations, and the six of us would do whatever we could to make sure it didn't crash and burn on our watch, with no help from our father.

"I know." I ran a hand over my jaw, resting my head back on the couch cushions. "I'll handle Luna, all right? She filed some bullshit paperwork that's going to pause progress on the demolition for a bit anyway. It's a waste of time and resources for us, but it should keep her out of trouble until we've secured our place in the article, at least."

"Well, that's great for a temporary solution, but how exactly are you going to handle her otherwise? You can't just handcuff her anytime you want."

The image of her on my bed, hands stretched over her head and handcuffed to the headboard, popped into my mind, and I had to bite back a groan. Whether it was of frustration or need, I didn't know. The two seemed to coalesce whenever my thoughts turned to her.

"I'll figure it out."

Regardless of what I did, I just needed to keep my head straight when it came to her. Especially if I was going to be around her when I didn't have the badge between us. I'd never once been in her presence out of my uniform, and I'd have preferred to keep it that way.

Too bad I wasn't going to get my wish.

CHAPTER SEVEN

LUNA

THIS WEEK HADN'T GONE EXACTLY as expected. Rain had been a blessing and a curse—it had kept any deforestation from happening, but it had also kept me from leading any yoga classes outside. And without any guests currently staying at the resort, I'd run through my sequences by myself in the parlor overlooking the ocean. It wasn't as good as outside, but I was going to take advantage of the space, considering I couldn't exactly practice in my van.

Today, though. Today was the day. It was unseasonably warm outside, which normally meant I'd be up at the crack of dawn, chaining myself to that huge tree to halt progress, but Brady had held up his end of the bargain—much to my shock—and the motion for discovery had been pushed through. Progress on the razing of the land had been halted—for now—as they investigated the property. And I'd never felt prouder.

Look at me, doing shit. Helping to make a change and a difference in the world. First, stopping the deforestation of this beautiful town. Next up: pulling the stick out from Grumpy's ass.

Since this would be my first official outdoor class in Starlight Cove, I wanted it to make a splash. Be an event. Something that actually drew people into the resort since there was no denying how bad off they were. So I'd asked around and gotten in touch with a local farmer who was all too willing to lend her baby goats to the cause in exchange for a few massages. Bartering was totally doable —was, in fact, my preferred means of payment and why my savings hadn't taken much of a hit since I'd settled into van life. Turned out there wasn't much people wouldn't do for a massage they didn't have to pay for.

And, yeah, so when I'd texted Brady a time to be at the resort for his first yoga class, I *may* have left off the tiny detail of this being yoga with farm animals. But there was no way he would've come if I'd been upfront about it. Better to beg for forgiveness and all that.

First thing that morning, I'd swung by Jane's farm to pick up the equipment I needed for a temporary enclosure. I'd love if this could be a standard offering at the resort, even if it happened after I was long gone—Addison had already registered half a dozen people, thanks to the sign I'd posted in town—which meant I needed to make sure this went off without a hitch.

I was usually a night owl, always had been, so today was going to be challenging, considering I'd woken up early and had slept like shit last night—and the several previous nights—my dreams consumed by one Sheriff Grumpy Pants. But I'd make do and find my Zen—while also definitely *not* thinking about the kiss that had ruined me. Or all the dreams I'd been having that'd had no qualms hypothesizing what might've happened if we hadn't stopped.

After dragging all the equipment out of my van, I stood, hands on hips, staring at the location Addison had suggested we put the enclosure. The space was tucked in a little area along the main path that wove through the entire resort. It was bracketed by trees and away from any cottages, but still close enough to the shore that the sounds of the crashing waves washed over me.

I pulled out my phone, glancing at the cracked screen for the time. I had a few hours yet before class started, but considering I was setting up the temporary enclosure on my own, I needed to get started. Addison hadn't been sold on something so out of the box—which meant Aiden *definitely* hadn't been—so this was all on me. Even if I'd never so much as hammered a nail in my life.

After two hours, one mishap with a mallet, a few splinters, and a stubbed toe, the enclosure was up and I was just laying out the mats when a throat cleared behind me. Beck and Ford stood outside the makeshift fence, eyebrows raised and arms crossed, looking like...well, twins. I still had no problem telling them apart, though. Besides the dead giveaway of the backward baseball cap Beck wore constantly, there was also the perpetual smirk on Ford's lips that Beck couldn't replicate if his life depended on it.

"You need some help?" Beck asked. "For the record, I'm volunteering him." He jerked a thumb toward his brother.

Ford shot me a smile—one that almost definitely got him laid plenty around town, but for some reason didn't do anything for me—and nodded. "Happy to help. Just tell me where you want me."

I opened my mouth to respond and tell them I had it handled, but before I could, Brady strode up, his jaw firm as he darted his gaze between his brothers and me.

"Those lines really work for you?" he asked Ford.

"Usually. Luna's a tough nut to crack, though." Ford winked at me. "But I'll keep trying."

Brady just grunted, narrowing his eyes on Beck before turning back to me. He lifted his chin toward the enclosure surrounding me. "You afraid I'm going to escape?"

The question was an easy one to answer—yes, obviously—but the words wouldn't come. Not when he'd struck me speechless, showing up here looking all kinds of indecent in basketball shorts and a tight white T-shirt that clung to his obscene muscles. Something so simple shouldn't look positively sinful on him, but there was no denying it did, especially considering I'd never seen him out of uniform. No denying how much I liked it, either. A lot. Definitely more than was advised of the person who kept arresting me.

Clearing my throat, I shook my head, my gaze torn away from the three larger-than-life McKenzie men—Jesus, what was in the water around here?—and to the large truck bouncing its way down the road. "Maybe a little, but this is for them." I lifted my chin toward the truck as it pulled to a stop behind the McKenzie brothers.

As if choreographed, all three men turned to look over their shoulders before regarding me with various expressions. Ford looked downright gleeful, Beck smug, and Brady looked wary. As he should.

Jane jumped down from the driver's side and offered a wave. "Hey, Luna! Glad to see you got that all set up. Let me just open up this back end, and we can get the sweet babies in there for your little event."

"What 'little event' is she talking about?" Brady asked, his tone heavy with wariness. "Something happening later today?"

"Not exactly." I shot him my best and brightest smile and swept an arm out to encompass the area I'd just set up. "It's for this."

Brady's eyes narrowed, but it was his brothers who figured it out first. Beck snorted at the same time Ford let out a loud bark of laughter.

"And you signed up for this?" Ford smacked Brady on

his chest. "Does Addison know? This would be perfect for the resort video footage."

"Not happening." Brady leveled me with a stare, his thick arms crossed and jaw set.

My nipples were standing at attention, and I couldn't think about what he was doing to things south of the border. Oh, he definitely had that whole intimidating man thing down—something I normally wasn't into, but my body positively lit up for when Brady was the one dishing it out—and it wasn't any less potent when all six foot, three inches of him was wrapped up in a T-shirt and shorts instead of his uniform.

But I didn't intimidate easily. My parents had taught me early to stand my ground. To not give in to the whims of anyone unless I wanted to, even if that *anyone* was a man twice my size. And if I could do that with the partners in my dad's law firm, who were stern and harsh, unaccustomed to not getting their way, then I could certainly do it with one grumpy small-town sheriff.

I tipped my head to the side and stepped toward them, stopping just on the other side of the enclosure. "Don't tell me you're scared of some baby goats."

His eye twitched, but that was the only tell that this was getting to him. "Depends on what those baby goats are doing."

"Yoga, obviously." I gestured behind me to the mats spaced evenly throughout the area.

He just continued staring then finally gave a firm, solid

shake of his head. "There's no way I'm getting in there with those things."

I shrugged. "Then the deal's off."

Brady's jaw ticked, his gaze dropping to my lips before heating just long enough for me to wonder if I'd imagined it. With narrowed eyes, he said, "After the other day, the deal's definitely not off."

Beck divided a look between us. "What happened the other day?"

"Yeah, I'd like to know, too." Ford propped his elbow on Beck's shoulder, his permanent grin firmly in place. "I promise I won't tattle to Mabel."

Brady ignored them both and shook his head at me. "I think you're making this up. There's no such thing as goat yoga."

I huffed out an indignant breath even as the goats came over in search of attention, their heads butting my legs and hands. "There is too! Look it up."

"That's a great idea." Brady stepped back, eyeing the animals warily. "I'll head home and do that now."

I rolled my eyes and looked at the twins. "Does he always whine this much?"

Ford nodded and said, "Yep," at the same time Beck said, "Pretty much."

Brady narrowed his eyes at his brothers, then at the innocent baby animals in the enclosure with me. "You get in there with them, then."

"Pass." Ford shook his head and took a giant step back.

Beck mimicked his twin. "Yeah, not gonna happen. I have to get back to the diner, and I'm pretty sure being around those animals before cooking would break several health codes."

My eyebrows lifted as I regarded all three of these grown-ass men who looked as if they'd rather jump off the bluffs and into the ocean than step in here with me. "Seriously?" I asked all three of them before pinning my gaze on Brady. "You carry a gun for a living and actively chase the bad guys, but you're scared of some baby animals?"

"I'm not *scared* of them. I just don't like them."

"How can you not? Look at these cute faces." I squatted down, laughing as a couple goats attempted to crawl up my body and one head-butted me.

Brady folded his arms over his chest and leveled me with a stare that did things no single look should have had the power of doing. "You're only saying that because you weren't here for the Goat Incident of 2017."

I snorted—I couldn't help it. Brady had delivered the line with as much weight as he would the report of a serial killer on the loose. "'The Goat Incident of 2017,' huh? Sounds like the premise for a very boring documentary. Has Netflix gotten in touch yet?"

"No, but Mabel was all over it." Ford darted his gaze to Brady before returning it to me. "It was the talk of the town for at least three months after it happened. Betty's vegetable garden never recovered."

"Not to mention the knocked-over beehives," Beck said. "I had to use store-bought honey for months."

"It was pandemonium," Brady agreed.

I stood and rolled my eyes. "Only you would think a bunch of goats loose in town was pandemonium."

"He's just uneasy because of how many tried to head-butt him in the junk," Ford said with a shrug as he walked backward. "I've gotta run. Addison's got a list for me a mile long, but have fun with all that." He gestured toward the enclosure before turning around and heading in the direction of the main inn.

The mention of Brady's junk was all it took to have my gaze snapping to it like a magnet, remembering exactly how hard and solid he'd been against me during our kiss. He cleared his throat, and I shot my eyes up to his, my cheeks flaming over being caught ogling him. He pinned me with an unreadable gaze, one brow raised slightly, but there was no way I was explaining why I was looking in the general vicinity of his dick as if desperate for X-ray vision.

"Am I early?" a feminine voice asked, and I jumped at the interruption, as if I were a teen caught looking at porn. A woman walked toward us, her stride one that said she was on a mission. Her hair was pulled back in a ponytail, and she had a bright smile on her face.

"Late, actually," Beck grumbled.

"You're here for the class?" I asked, though that much was obvious by the rolled-up yoga mat she had slung over her shoulder.

"I am," she said, sticking out her hand for me. "I'm Everly. We haven't officially met yet."

"Luna," I said, returning her smile. "It's nice to meet you. Is this your first time with goats?"

"First time doing yoga, yes, but not my first time with goats. I'm the vet in town, so I was there for the birth of all these beauties. But I don't get nearly enough time with them. I skipped my morning jog so I wouldn't miss it."

Beck studied her, his gaze tracking over her from head to toe, as if to make sure she was still in working order. "When you didn't show up for your morning coffee, I was hoping it was something I said."

Everly laughed and patted his biceps. "So those twelve texts demanding to know where I was and that I was okay were just, what? Butt-dials?"

Beck grunted some semblance of a nonanswer before turning and stalking off, Everly's laugh directed at his retreating form.

I may have been new to town and didn't know all the ins and outs of the residents and their varied relationships, but there was no denying something was going on there. "What's that all about?"

"What? That?" Everly pointed to Beck's retreating form then shrugged. "Beck being Beck."

"Why do you care what's going on with them?" Brady asked, a hard edge to his voice that was ever-present around me.

"Oh good, I see you brought your bad attitude to class

so we can work through that with some deep breathing." I grinned at him, gesturing toward the makeshift gate. "You're wasting time, Sheriff."

"Aren't we waiting for the rest of your class?"

"We're here!" Mabel called, waving her hand wildly as she hurried down the path, three other gray-haired ladies trailing after her, all wearing spandex. "Save me a mat, would you? I just need to do a quick intro."

She fumbled with her phone before holding it out in front of her, her back to me as she spoke to the screen.

"Seriously?" Brady said as he held open the gate for the other newcomers to enter in front of him. "I don't think yoga necessitates a Facebook Live, Mabel."

I snorted, knowing full well how much he loathed the older woman's penchant for getting in the way of official business with her special brand of reporting. And let me tell you, I was here for it.

"It's *goat* yoga, thank you very much." Mabel sniffed, sliding her phone into her pocket. "Besides, I thought you'd be all for a Live that showcases more of your family's resort. Am I wrong?"

Brady grumbled something under his breath that sounded a lot like *nosy old woman is going to be the death of me*, but before I could call him on it, he stepped into the enclosure and shut the makeshift gate behind him. With his eyes tracking the erratic movements of the baby goats, he strolled straight for a mat at the back, but I shook my head before he got settled.

"Not so fast, Sheriff. I saved you a spot. Right up front." I gestured to the mat directly in front of me.

Brady's eyes locked with mine, and that ever-present zing of awareness shot through me, turning my nipples to hard points against my thin top. Okay, so this maybe wasn't my best idea, but there was no way I was going to let him slack off at the back of the class. Not with what I'd given up for this deal.

"Show us how it's done, Sheriff!" Mabel called, her friends clapping their encouragement. "I promise to only take video of you if it's flattering. But considering what you're working with, I don't think that's going to be a problem. You know that video I made of you directing traffic with your derrière pointed my direction still holds the record for highest views, right? Imagine what a video of you doing yoga will accomplish! Probably, you should take your shirt off. The classes will be booked out for months."

"That sounds like a *very* interesting video, Mabel," I said. "I guess I know what I'll be doing tonight."

He shot me a look that said *don't you dare*, and I just grinned in response, settling into place at the front even as the goats roamed around, eating grass—and hair—or burrowing in for cuddles. "Thanks for coming, everyone. How many of you have taken a yoga class before?"

Only one hand rose—Everly's—though I wasn't surprised.

I nodded and settled onto my mat in Sukhasana and gestured for everyone to do the same. "This class will be a fun one to start with. If you're looking for something a bit more structured, be sure to stop by the main inn and grab a schedule from Addison for the standard classes I run."

With that, I began the class, guiding them through their practice and walking around to help correct poses when needed. While older, Mabel and her friends were surprisingly limber and able to do most of the poses with little direction from me—because of all the sex, she'd stated with a wink.

Brady had just grunted at that—whether from Mabel's statement or the goats that flocked to him, I wasn't sure. He definitely needed the most help of this group. The guy was a mess, though that wasn't a surprise, considering he looked more like an Avenger than he did a yogi.

I squatted next to him as he attempted a balancing table pose, and I tipped my head until I could meet his eyes. "Need some help, Sheriff?"

"I'm fine," he grumbled, even as two goats pounced on his back, a third attempting to jump up as well.

"Actually, you're getting a little droopy. Do you mind?" I held up my hands and gestured to his core.

He grunted. "Can't get any worse."

I wasn't so sure about that, but I slid my hand between the goats to press a palm on his back, the other on his abs —abs I could've gone my whole life without knowing how hard and solid they were. How hot his skin was under my touch. Why the hell had I offered to help him hold this pose?

Right. Because it was my job. A job I needed to focus on.

"If these goats weren't on me—"

"You'd still have this problem." I smiled, though it died on my lips when he turned his face toward mine, our noses so close I could feel his breath sweep across my mouth. When he was quiet like this, just his gorgeous green gaze boring into me and enough electricity between us to power a small country, it was easy to forget our differences and why I absolutely should not close the distance between us and remind myself what he tasted like.

Before I could do anything I'd regret, one of the baby goats burrowed her way between us, bopping me with her nose before she, too, tried to climb up on the Brady train, desperate for a ride on the sheriff.

Me too, girl. Me too.

Needing to avoid any further missteps, I made sure to pay extra attention to the rest of the ladies, even completing an impromptu Facebook Live interview courtesy of Mabel when class had wrapped up. Anything to keep busy and away from the grump who'd somehow snagged my—and my libido's—attention.

I'd led hundreds of yoga classes, and I'd never—not once—been attracted to a client. Not like this. And certainly not to a man like Brady.

But I'd gotten myself into this because, as usual, I'd leaped before I looked. So not only was I going to have to do this all over again with him—and without the convenient interruption of the baby animals—but there was still the matter of that massage…

After all the other attendees left, Brady, for all his goat bluster and bad attitude, helped Jane load the animals back into the truck before sending her off with a double pat to the truck bed and a wave.

I squinted up at him when he stepped in front of me, the sun peeking out behind his tousled hair. "How was it?"

"Exactly as bad as I thought it'd be," he said, reaching out to pluck something from my hair. He held the blade of grass up between us before releasing it into the breeze. "And not nearly as relaxing as you promised."

His gaze dropped to my lips, and the heat between us ratcheted up another dozen or so notches, officially sending it into the stratosphere. There was no denying whatever I was feeling wasn't one-sided.

I just didn't know if that made this special hell we were in better or worse.

CHAPTER EIGHT

BRADY

SINCE IT WAS my day off and I was already at the resort, I figured I might as well swing by the diner and grab something to eat. Even if it meant taking a ribbing from one or more of my brothers on the fact that I'd had to endure those damn goats. Didn't matter. In fact, it might help. God knew I needed something to focus on to get my mind off Luna and her hands on me.

Why the hell had I given her the green light to touch me? Especially when she'd been wearing *that*—a pair of leggings that showcased her perfect ass and a thin shirt that left little to the imagination swooping low over one shoulder. It showed off the tiny strap of a pale-pink tank top and the black lines of a dainty tattoo in the shape of a constellation that stretched across her left shoulder, just over her collarbone. I had no doubt the damn thing would make an appearance in my dreams tonight, along with the remembered feel of her hands on me, and the coconut-lime scent of her hair that made me hard for no goddamn good reason.

I pulled open the door to the diner, pleased to see a couple I didn't know at one of the three tables and Jon, the owner of the hardware store, taking up another. Three people buying lunch wouldn't exactly spark life back into this place, but it was better than nothing.

Jon and I exchanged nods as I settled at the bar, running a hand through my hair as Beck stepped up and slid me a glass of water.

"How was it?" he asked.

I grunted then drained the glass. "Never thought I'd need to wear a cup for yoga, so there's that."

Beck snorted, leaning back against the counter behind him, his arms and ankles crossed as he regarded me. "Well, *I* definitely had fun. Thanks for the entertainment."

He and half of Starlight Cove, thanks to Mabel, her nuisance of a phone, and her penchant for causing trouble.

"Yeah, well, thanks for lunch."

"What lunch?"

"You know what I like. I'll wait."

Beck just shook his head, turning his back to me as he pulled out ingredients. "It's really a wonder why you're still single," he said dryly.

Considering my job was a very close second on my list of priorities right after my family, and my life always consisted of issues from one or the other, no. It really wasn't a wonder. No one wanted to be third place after a job that took too much of my time and a family that took even more. I was thirty-five years old and had never had a relationship—long-term, short-term, extended booty call, or otherwise. I'd never allowed anyone past the wall I'd erected a long time ago, and no one had ever cared enough to try.

"Could say the same about you."

Beck grunted and set a plate down in front of me as he waved to someone outside the diner. Considering we had all of...zero guests staying at the resort, I twisted on the barstool and glanced out the front windows to see who it was.

Luna. Of course, because I couldn't get away from her.

She smiled at Beck, lifting her hand in a wave as she strolled down the path toward the main inn. The tiny niggle that had been consistently getting louder by the day was nearly a siren now as I darted my gaze between my brother and the woman who drove me out of my mind. The woman whose lips I could still taste and whose fiery eyes and undeniable spark lit something inside me I'd long thought dead.

Nothing good would come of voicing this question, no matter what the answer was. But I still couldn't seem to keep it bottled up.

I twisted back in my seat and picked up half of my sandwich. "There something going on with you two?

"Who?" he asked, brows drawn. "Me and Luna? No, why?"

I took a large bite, taking out a third of it in a single go and ignoring the sudden wash of relief that swept over me. Shrugging, as if the answer didn't bother me one way or another, I said, "You know her order..."

Beck's eyebrows flew up his forehead, nearly to the bottom of his backward baseball cap. "I know everyone's orders. Kind of goes with the territory." He gestured to the tuna salad on wheat in front of me. "I know yours, Luna's, Jon's, Everly's... Does that mean I'm into them, too?"

"You go out of your way for Luna."

"I cook for her. It's literally my job. How is that going out of my way?"

"You're stocking all kinds of disgusting shit in here now, all because she asked you to."

"No, she *suggested* some varied offerings that would appeal to a broader range of customers while also allowing us to keep our supplies local." He braced himself on the counter in front of me. "There's a big difference between going out of my way for someone and taking their suggestions into consideration because it makes good business sense."

I stuffed the last of my sandwich into my mouth and studied him, looking for any kind of tell but coming up empty. "So...nothing?"

"Not even a little. Why, you into her?"

I'd just taken a drink and promptly choked on my

water, coughing and sputtering as I glared at him. I swiped the back of my hand over my mouth. "Of course not. She's impossible. She's too cheerful. Too unpredictable. Too…"

"Unencumbered by rules?"

"Exactly. She drives me up a wall. I want to strangle her half the time."

"And the other half?"

I snapped my jaw shut, even as he stared at me with a knowing glint in his eye. Like he knew the other half was fantasies of handcuffing her to my bed and giving her mouth something else to do besides running a mile a minute and driving me crazy.

Beck knocked twice on the counter before grabbing the pitcher of water and refilling my glass. "Yep, that checks."

"What checks?"

He stared at me for a long moment before shaking his head. "You seriously don't get what's going on here? It's a classic case of opposites attract."

"Of what?"

"*Opposites attract*," he enunciated. "You know, where, on paper, two people couldn't be less of a match, but in person—" he brought his hands up, miming an explosion "—sparks fly.

"Are you drunk right now?"

"No, I'm not fucking drunk. And don't act like *I'm* the idiot out of the two of us. Maybe you should read more. It's a very popular romance novel trope."

"A…romance novel trope," I said slowly. "Is that what

you've been doing in here?"

"Whatever. Everly reads, like, two a week. Can't get enough of 'em. She left one here, and I had to know what the appeal was. It was the off-season, and I was bored. What do you do when you're bored?"

"Set some speed traps. At least my boredom brings valuable dollars into the town."

Beck rolled his eyes. "All I'm saying is one of us is right. And one of us is about to fall for his complete opposite, if it hasn't happened already."

"You didn't tell me you were going to ask out Everly."

He snorted. "Nice try. Opposites as she and I may be, there's no friends-to-lovers in our future, but there definitely could be some enemies-to-lovers in yours."

"You're really starting to worry me. Do I need to stage an intervention?"

Beck snatched my empty plate and tossed it into the bin below the counter, fixing me with a hard stare. "Make jokes all you want, but don't come crying to me when you need help with a grand gesture."

"A grand—what?" I held up my hand as I stood, shaking my head. "You know what? Never mind. I'll see you later."

I had no idea why the fact that there was nothing going on with Beck and Luna had loosened something in my chest. Settled the undercurrent that had been bubbling for days. Had no idea why I cared enough to ask in the first place.

A FEW DAYS had passed since I'd last seen Luna, and that was exactly how I preferred it. The motion for discovery that she'd filed was holding up progress for Holton Group, which meant I hadn't had to babysit her to ensure she wasn't causing trouble.

But that didn't mean I wasn't keenly aware of every move she made in town. I had no choice in the matter, considering the busybodies of Starlight Cove and their penchant for sticking their noses where they didn't belong. Why they thought I'd want to know she'd stopped by the senior center to give complimentary massages to the residents or made a house call to ninety-three-year-old Greta bearing a homemade foot cream to help with her neuropathy was beyond me.

I had enough on my plate to worry about, and what Luna spent her time doing wasn't on that very extensive list, so long as she kept her nose out of trouble and her wrists out of my cuffs.

"Good news," Addison said as soon as everyone was seated at the dining table. It was usually too early for her to do much but grumble during these meetings, let alone smile, but there was no denying the grin stretched wide across her mouth. "Well, sort of. I just got an email."

"Thanks for sharing," Aiden said dryly, never lifting his gaze from his phone, "but we don't actually need to know the contents of your inbox."

"An *email*," she continued as if he hadn't spoken, "that said while they haven't made their decision yet—"

"Who's 'they'?" Ford asked, pulling the top off one of the muffins Beck had brought before stuffing the whole thing in his mouth.

She shot him an exasperated look. "*Weekend Wanderlust.*"

Aiden straightened up. "Did we get it?"

"If you idiots would let me speak, I could tell you." Addison pinned us each with a look, and when we all kept our mouths shut, she finally said, "They've narrowed their selection down for the feature, and the last spot is between us and one other town."

"That's..." Disappointing? Frustrating? A kick in the nuts?

"Yeah," she agreed with a nod. "But it's not a no, so I'm keeping the faith. They're sending someone back to observe the festival this weekend."

"Harper?" I asked, brow raised.

"Yep, she's checking in on Thursday."

"Wait..." Beck said, brows drawn. "Harper who used to spend every summer here, glued to Levi's side? That Harper?"

"One and the same," Addison confirmed with a nod.

"Since we're trying to get on her good side, don't mention Levi around her," I said before taking a sip of my coffee. "Made that mistake already. Apparently they tossed out their friendship bracelets."

"Noted," Beck muttered with a nod.

"Hopefully this storm doesn't fuck up her arrival." Aiden thumbed his phone, probably scrolling for the latest weather update.

A storm had cropped up, gaining more traction than what we usually saw this time of the year, but it still wasn't much to worry about. As of now, the forecasters had issued a high wind and coastal flood watch, but it hadn't even escalated to a warning yet. It'd probably die down into nothing and fizzle out before it reached us.

I waved him off. "She'll be fine."

"Which cottage are we putting her in while she's here?" Aiden asked, glancing up at Addison.

"One, obviously."

The resort property was spread out over five acres and contained the main inn—which didn't actually offer any guest rooms since it was where Addison and Aiden lived—as well as nineteen cottages along the shore, some directly on the beach and others on the bluffs. No two were alike, and whether intentional or not, we'd focused most of our efforts on the lower numbers in recent years—the ones with the best locations and interiors—and let anything above ten languish. Cottage Nineteen was practically a storage unit now, stuffed with all the castoffs we didn't have a place for, and Ford had moved in to Cottage Sixteen, not wanting to wake Aiden or Addison with any late-night emergency calls—not to say anything of the unmentionable Cottage Thirteen—though it wasn't like it mattered. We hadn't had more than five cottages booked at the same time in years.

"I'm going to spend the rest of the week working through our list and making sure everything's in order," Addison said. "Ford, I could use your help."

He saluted her. "You got it, boss."

"Between the festival and everything else, Harper's weekend will be full. I've already talked with Luna—she's going to run a one-on-one yoga class for Harper while she's here, and we've got Cottage Two set up for a massage. I know we did this as a compromise with her, but I'd love if this could be a permanent offering for the resort, and I think a write-up about it would really help."

The mention of a massage reminded me that I still had part of my deal to make good on, and it soured me all over again. "Since you're actively inviting Luna into Harper's presence, I take it I'm off the hook?"

Addison laughed. "No, you definitely still need to keep an eye on her. You just don't need to do it while she's on the clock here. It's her downtime I worry about, and we don't need any more surprises. Not when this isn't a sure thing yet."

Yeah, if only it was that easy. Trouble was, Luna was full of surprises, and I feared that no matter how much I looked after her, and no matter how much I attempted to keep her under my thumb, we'd still be caught off guard at one point or another.

CHAPTER NINE

BRADY

THE REST OF THE WEEK, I'd kept my ear close to the news, listening for updates on the storm moving in. I'd figured it was going to fizzle out to nothing before it reached us, but it'd only gotten worse. As the week had worn on, the storm watches had escalated to warnings, and the ocean was an angry, writhing mess, crashing against the shore with a vengeance.

The possibility of this storm being a high risk for casualties and steep damages was slim to none. A nuisance, yes. Probable lost power? Also yes. But life-or-death it was not. So then, why the hell was my chest so tight?

That morning, we'd switched to our alpha/bravo shifts in deference to the storm warnings, and Deputy Traeger was already at the station, having relieved me from my day shift. Harper had made it to the resort a few hours ago and was settled in her cottage, ready to move to the inn if need be. All but a few businesses in town had decided to close a couple hours early so they could ride out the storm at their homes. I'd checked on the elderly residents who lived on their own, making sure they had everything they needed, as well as verifying a couple of the churches in town were set up as shelters, just in case. And I'd made a pass through the preserve that morning to warn any campers of the impending storm, and what few were there had cleared out.

All except Luna.

She hadn't been there when I'd shown up, and a quick peek through the windows showed she'd left her van unlocked in her absence. I'd opened it to find nothing left of her but a faint hint of lavender and jasmine in the air and promptly slammed the door shut—as well as any reaction my body had to her mouthwatering scent. I should've left a note inside or taken one of the two dozen colored rocks she'd had lining her dashboard just to prove a point that she was leaving herself wide open to who knew what when she did shit like that. Honestly, did this woman have a daily quota of how much she needed to frustrate me?

Regardless of how irritating she was, it was my duty as the county sheriff to make sure she was safe. I'd do the same for any other Starlight Cove resident or visitor. Which meant I certainly couldn't leave her out there in her sardine can of a "home" to ride out this storm, obstinate, infuriating woman or not.

I sat in my patrol car parked on the dirt road that led to

the preserve, protected from the rain battering the windshield. Along the bluff at the far edge of the area, waves crashed so hard, spray still arced over the fifteen feet of rock jutting up from the shore. And somewhere in there, too damn close to the unpredictability of the ocean, was Luna.

Clenching my jaw, I pulled out my phone and pressed Addison's name, reassuring myself that I'd do this for anyone, not just the newcomer who had a knack for getting under my skin.

"Hey, everything okay?" Addison asked.

"Fine." I cleared my throat. "Luna needs a cottage."

"She...what?"

"Needs a cottage."

"Well," she said, drawing out the word, "we're not really in the market for giving away free cottages."

"What, it's a prerequisite they're a lost soul from Mississippi before you'll consider it?" I asked, referring to the visitor we'd had recently who'd wasted my time with a bullshit grand theft situation.

Addison sniffed. "That was different. Her car was stolen—"

"*Borrowed.*"

"And she didn't have a purse, let alone any money. What was I supposed to do?"

"I could ask you the same thing."

She sighed heavily. "I'm just not so sure it's a great idea. She'll already be here around Harper during working hours, and that's enough to worry about. Remember what I said about her downtime and surprises?"

I ground my teeth together, the undeniability of Addison's words battling with this newly present and completely unwanted urge to make sure Luna was safe. "She's in a fucking van during a Nor'easter, Addison, and she's parked twenty yards from the ocean."

Addison breathed out a heavy sigh. "Look, I get where you're coming from, I do. But do you really think having Luna here...at the resort...around a journalist we're trying to win over...is the best course of action, considering everything we're trying to accomplish?"

Dammit, no. It wasn't. We needed this article—needed it to paint the resort in a complimentary light—and Luna was a wild card. No question about that. And no telling what kind of havoc she'd have swirling around her.

"What the hell do you suggest I do, then? I can't just leave her out there. It's not safe."

"Let her stay at your place if you're so worried about it," she said, and I could practically hear her shrug through the phone. "You know you're just going straight back to the station to make sure everything's done *properly* anyway, even if you're supposed to be off duty."

I kept my mouth shut, because, yeah, that had been my plan.

"For what it's worth, though," she continued, "I think this is totally unnecessary. You know the storm's not going to get that bad. Plus, she's an adult and can take care of herself."

Of that, I wasn't so sure. Who knew how often she left her doors unlocked? Not to mention, her tires were constantly low, and there was no doubt she drove around on a sixteenth of a tank of gas, just for the hell of it. God knew what I'd find if I checked her oil. She had no sense of self-preservation—hell, I wouldn't be surprised if she was outside right now, exposed to all the elements, just so she could become one with the rain or whatever the fuck.

My chest grew tighter at the thought, recalling the tourist who'd drowned a few years ago just half a mile from where Luna was parked. She and a group of friends had been standing on some rocks overlooking the ocean, watching the angry swell of the waves as a storm had rolled in. But they'd been too close to the edge. She'd been caught off guard by a huge wave that'd come out of nowhere and swept her straight into the ocean.

That was it. No warning. No mercy. Just gone forever. And no one could do a damn thing about it.

No matter how good of a swimmer you were, no matter if you were a world-class sailor or if you'd lived your entire life steps from the ocean, you weren't immune to its unpredictability or its ruthlessness.

"Plus," Addison said, "taking her farther from the resort can only be a good thing while we're trying to secure this, right?"

Fuck. I rubbed at the pressure in my chest, hating that

she was right. Which left me with one option. The rest of my family, save for Levi, lived on the resort, and I sure as fuck wasn't going to send Luna to his apartment. The last thing any of us needed was those two troublemakers concocting a plan together. God help us all if that ever happened.

I'd swing by her van, let her know the situation, and take her to my place. She could stay there—alone—until the storm passed, while I hunkered down at the station. And then, when it was clear, she could return to her hippie van and continue ruining my life from afar.

After verifying Addison was in for the night and ending the call, I put the car into drive and headed down the path, wipers on full speed to keep up with the downpour. The wind had already ravaged parts of the preserve, and branches were down all over the place, my headlights skating over several littering the road.

Christ, she was far in here—far enough that no one would even know it if they hadn't been looking specifically for her. That was trouble all around.

I was about fifty yards from her van when a downed tree blocked my path. It was massive—big enough that it'd take several people several hours and a chainsaw to clear it. And considering this was the only road in and out of the preserve and she'd parked at the very end of the dead-end path, that meant she was trapped.

My ire kicked up when I thought about what she'd have done if I hadn't come out here and she'd had an emergency, or if the storm had picked up more power, increasing the likelihood of damage. She'd have been stuck with no way out. And the thought only pissed me off more. Was she just oblivious, or did she truly lack even an ounce of self-preservation?

It probably wasn't a good idea to go in guns blazing and barking orders, but she had me so worked up by her total disregard for her safety, it took effort to unclench my jaw as I climbed out of the car.

The rain soaked me in seconds as I strode toward her pale-blue van, my headlights illuminating the way. I didn't realize how much I'd been hoping she was inside seeking the minuscule protection the vehicle offered until my shoulders went stiff when I found her. Outside, just as I'd thought. She stood under the poor excuse for cover the trees provided, just staring out at the raging sea, a small smile tipping her lips as the wind whipped her hair into a tornado around her.

I stalked up to her, running my gaze over every inch and checking for any injuries. She stood in bare feet—*bare fucking feet*—her long skirt whipping in the wind, and wore a cardigan over a too-thin shirt, the rain making it stick to her curves in ways that should have been illegal.

Snapping my eyes away from her body, I met her curious gaze. "Let's go," I said, loud enough to be heard over the storm and the sound of the angry ocean.

She regarded me with upturned lips so plush they were distracting, droplets of rain cascading over them and making my fingers itch to reach out and wipe them away. "Hello to you, too, grump."

I made a gruff sound in my throat, clenching my fists to keep myself from reaching for her and throwing her over my shoulder to get the hell out of here. "We don't have time for niceties."

She breathed out a laugh that I saw more than heard and shook her head. "Is that what you call the bare minimum of civility?"

Jesus Christ, this woman. It was like she got off on pushing my buttons. Were there any circumstances we wouldn't be at each other's throats?

"It's not safe to stay in your van," I bit out through gritted teeth.

"It's fine, Sheriff." She reached out and patted my chest, the chill of her hand seeping into my skin, even through my uniform. "I'm a big girl and can take care of myself."

I reached up and caught her hand under mine. It was like covering an ice cube, and I narrowed my eyes, wondering how long she'd been out here like this to be so cold. Was the rest of her body just as chilled? "Big girls usually remember to lock their doors, so I'm not so sure about that."

She rolled her eyes, but she didn't remove her hand as she leaned closer so she wouldn't have to yell to be heard. "I didn't *forget*. I just...didn't."

Rain had gathered on the tips of her eyelashes, and every blink sent a droplet streaming down the slope of her nose, over the curve of her cheek, before pooling into the dip of the Cupid's bow on her mouth. A cupid's bow I wanted to trace the shape of. With my tongue. My gaze was stuck there, even as my frustration ratcheted up another notch at her total disregard for her safety.

I tore my eyes away and met her gaze. "You mean to tell me it was an *active* choice to leave your van open for anyone to slip inside? Do you leave it unlocked while you're sleeping, too?"

She averted her eyes, which told me all I needed to know, and that only pissed me off more.

"You've got to be kidding me."

"I don't do it *all* the time."

"That doesn't make it better," I said through clenched teeth.

"Whatever. You're not here about my unlocked doors. Or is there some law I broke that I'm not aware of?"

"I'm here because of the weather." *And because you can't be left to your own devices*, though I kept that part to myself.

"I think I can make it through one little storm," she said, trying to pull her hand free, but I tightened my grip, refusing to let her go.

"This isn't just 'one little storm,' Luna. People die in these storms."

The words sat bitter on my tongue, the memory of that tourist from last year combined with what had happened to our family so long ago—one small choice that had led to catastrophic consequences—cropping up anew.

"I think you're overreacting," she said with an eye roll.

I pinched the bridge of my nose and attempted to do the breathing exercise Ford had shown me. I made it a single breath in before snapping, "And I think you're a pain in my ass. So what the fuck else is new?"

Note to self: breathing exercises do not work when faced with an adversary like Luna.

She inhaled deeply and peeled my hand away before tucking hers into her cardigan pocket. "I appreciate your concern, Sheriff, but I've been just fine so far, and I've been on my own for a long time."

"You're kidding, right?" I asked in disbelief. "If you haven't had anything happen, that's pure dumb luck. And you're due." I gestured to the thick tree trunk blocking her path out, nearly as large as the gigantic tree she'd chained herself to the week before. "Clearly. That fallen tree means you're stuck out here until it's safe to break it down, and that's not going to happen until the storm passes and the main streets in town are cleared of any fallen debris. Which means even if something happens and you *need* to leave, there's no getting out."

"Why would I need to leave?"

"Jesus, I don't know," I said, throwing up my hands. "You run out of food or water. A gust of wind knocks another tree over, but this one falls right on your van. You overdose on essential oils. Truly, the list is endless when it comes to you."

She shot me an unimpressed look out of the corner of her eyes. "Your faith in me is astounding."

I clenched my jaw, speaking through my teeth. "I'm not joking. Now, get in the goddamn car."

Chin jutted up, she crossed her arms over her chest, the move plastering her already fitted tee to her skin, her tits pressed up, nipples high and tight. "The only way I'm getting in that car is if you handcuff me and force me in."

I narrowed my eyes on her before sweeping my gaze over her from head to toe, letting my stare linger in a way I swore I wouldn't again. Not after that kiss. Not after her soft little moans got my dick so hard it was painful. Not after she'd consumed every night's dreams since. Not after I'd only been able to picture her every time I beat off. But my intentions didn't matter when the rush of finding her safe while she was still in danger was consuming me. Bubbling under my skin and demanding I *do* something. And that had nothing on the way this woman goaded me... challenged me... It did something to me that no one else had managed to before.

Crack me.

Finally meeting her gaze, I stepped up to her, close enough that she had to tip her head back to look up at me, and swept my thumb across her lower lip, catching a rain droplet. "Don't tempt me, lawbreaker."

This close, I could make out the starburst around her irises, a ring of fire in that bottomless blue. Could make out the half a dozen freckles dotting her nose, even as rain speckled her skin. Could make out the rough rise and fall of her chest as she regarded me with parted lips.

She blinked up at me through the downpour, hair plastered to her skin, and held up her hands between us. "Do it, then," she said, her voice low and gravelly, and the sound of it compounded with her demand shot straight to my cock.

Christ, the things I wanted to do to her. I wanted to cuff her hands behind her back, press her against the van, and lift up that wisp of a skirt before burying my tongue inside her pussy. Wanted my handprint left on her ass, a reminder of what an obstinate little thing she was. Wanted to drive into her so deep and use her cuffed wrists as leverage to work her back and forth over my cock until we both shuddered through our releases.

Just then, the sky lit up and a crack of thunder shook the ground, the winds whipping around us as another large branch fell only a dozen feet away. She jumped, bringing her body even closer to mine, until she was pressed right up against me. We were wasting time, and I didn't have a whole lot more restraint left in me. If we didn't hurry, we'd have to contend with downed trees as well as flooding as I attempted to navigate our way back to my house and get her to safety—if the path hadn't already been blocked while I'd been out here arguing with her.

So, I called her bluff.

Her lips parted as I pulled out my cuffs and slapped

one on her left hand. Then, with our eyes locked, I hooked the other one on my right wrist instead of hers.

Her lips parted in shock as she divided her wide-eyed stare between my eyes and our joined hands. "What the hell did you do that for?"

Lifting a brow, I said, "I'm not leaving you out here by yourself. So either we both go, or neither of us does."

She stared, mouth agape, to where we were connected. "You seriously just did that."

"Yep, I seriously just did. Now, what'll it be, lawbreaker?" I wrapped my left arm around her, pressing my palm to her lower back and holding her flush against me. "I can either drop you off at my place and head back into the station to be of service to the people who need it, or we can stay out here in your van. Your call."

CHAPTER TEN

LUNA

I GAVE IN.

But really, what choice did I have? With the way Brady
had stared down at me, all tight jaw and fierce eyes, shoulders big enough to make me feel like I was cocooned in
safety even amid the storm, I wasn't about to be held
responsible for what would happen if we'd stayed. Not to
mention that I'd been lulled into complacency by the heat
emanating from his body and how nice he'd felt all firm
and solid against me...

He'd hypnotized me with all his dumb man juju.

So now, I sat in the passenger's seat of his patrol car—
at least he'd let me sit up front this time—feeling all
kinds of mixed-up, not to mention soaking wet, as Brady
drove us toward his house. I'd intended to bask in the
rain and enjoy the storm for a bit before stripping down
in my van and curling up under a blanket with a good

romance novel until the sound of the rain lulled me to sleep.

All my good intentions were thwarted by a pissed-off grump of a man who was, for some unknown reason, dead set on ensuring my safety. If it weren't so frustrating, it'd be kind of...sweet. And so utterly different from what I was used to. Who knew he had it in him? And who knew his mantrum—a man tantrum, natch—focusing on my safety would be my particular brand of kryptonite?

If I'd come across Brady McKenzie years ago, I might have been swept up in all his posturing, but after a lifetime of relying on myself, I'd learned to trust my instincts. And they hadn't failed me yet.

Trouble was, my instincts seemed to be on the fritz when it came to the sheriff. One minute, I wanted to strangle him, and the next, I wanted to climb him like a tree and see what all that pent-up aggression would feel like in the bedroom. Obviously, neither of which was a smart choice. The first would mean decades in prison, and I wasn't made for life in heavy-duty lockup, despite how often I'd been arrested. There was no way they'd accommodate my locally harvested organic vegetarian meals, and I doubted they'd allow me to bring in my crystal collection.

And the second? Well. Brady wasn't the kind of guy who had impromptu sex with a woman who didn't have a 401(k) or even a set day of the week she went grocery shopping. He'd pair better with someone meek and docile. Someone who sat by quietly just waiting to please him, a softer, prettier version of a *yes-man*. Someone he could fit in a nice, neat little box, and that sure as hell wasn't me.

That didn't mean it was easy to ignore the potent sexual chemistry between us. Even now, as we sat next to each other in the car we'd been in plenty of times before, I couldn't deny it. The tension pulsed between us like a living, breathing entity. And if we didn't get out of this too-small space, I was afraid it'd swallow us both whole.

Thank God he was just dropping me off before heading back to the station. Some separation would do us good. Give us time to cool down and get our heads on straight.

"You have a change at the station?" I asked, my gaze tracking over him.

He white-knuckled the steering wheel, his jaw set while he glared at the roads as if they'd personally affronted him. Rainwater still slicked his forearms, his uniform plastered to him like a second skin. His hair was wet, a shaggy, rumpled mess that was so out of place on him, I nearly pulled out my phone to take a picture so there'd forever be proof of his dishevelment.

"What?" he asked, darting his gaze toward me before snapping it back to the road. Didn't matter, though. That second of eye contact was all it took for this tension between us to build even higher.

God, how could I be so attracted to this man who was

completely unbending, so consumed by control he couldn't let go for even a second?

"You're soaking wet," I said, leaving off the fact that he wasn't the only one... "So I just wondered if you have another uniform at the station to change into or if you'll change at your house."

I hoped to God he had something at the station and this would be a quick drop-off scenario. There was no telling what'd happen if we had to spend even more time together. We'd either rip off each other's heads or clothes. No telling, really.

He grunted, his eyes sweeping the roads. "I've got a backup at the station. And I'm not sure what I'll come across between my house and there, so I'll wait to get changed, in case I need to be out in this again."

The thought of him outside in this mess made my belly jump with nerves, but I wasn't about to examine that too closely. It was admirable, really, how he'd do whatever needed to be done to make sure others were safe. But who looked after him? Who made sure *he* was safe?

Starlight Cove was a ghost town as Brady drove us down Main Street. No one was out walking along the sidewalks; no cars were in the various parking lots we passed. Garbage cans were overturned thanks to the wind, and branches littered the streets.

A mile or two from the resort, Brady pulled onto a gravel road that I would've missed entirely if I'd been driving. No streetlights shone on the path, the only light illuminating our way the car's headlights as we bumped along the road. A thick cropping of trees loomed on either side of the gravel trail, closing us in, and there wasn't a house in sight.

"Did it finally happen?" I asked.

"Did what finally happen?"

I turned toward him, tucking my left leg under me as I twisted in the seat. "You snapped, and you're dragging me out to the middle of nowhere to murder me, aren't you?"

He huffed out something that sounded awfully close to a laugh, but that was impossible. I'd never seen the man so much as smile. "Not today."

Was he being...flirty? It was so far off our usual repertoire, I nearly didn't know what to do with myself. Nearly.

"Oh good," I said with a smile. "Maybe tomorrow, then. I'll warn you, though...I'm a screamer."

He pulled up in front of a cute Cape Cod home—the only one on this whole stretch of road—the car's headlights revealing light-colored shaker-style siding with dark shutters. The porch light was on, but the rain was so heavy, I couldn't see much past the steps leading down from the front door.

He slid his gaze to me, something dark and...heated?... hiding in those depths that had me shifting in my seat. "I'll have to test that statement some other time."

I shrugged as if I hadn't picked up on the tempestuous undercurrent between us. As if it wasn't making my pussy even wetter and my nipples even harder. "Just let me know.

I'll make sure I'm wearing panties. Don't want to give anyone a heart attack when they find me."

He froze for half a second, then turned to me, a single eyebrow raised, and yeah. I definitely wasn't imagining the heat in his eyes. "You have to plan to wear panties, lawbreaker?"

I lifted a single shoulder, suddenly feeling incredibly naked, even though all my bits and bobbles were covered by my clothes, wet as they were. What would he do if he found out today wasn't one of those planned days? "You have to get crafty when you don't have consistent access to a washing machine."

I could've sworn I heard him swear lowly under his breath, but a loud boom of thunder drowned him out, the flash of lightning through the sky highlighting his harsh, tight features for a second before plunging us back into darkness. He pulled his phone from his pocket, navigated to an app, and then a second later, his garage door opened.

Stacks of chopped wood lined each side, enough that he wouldn't run out for a solid three years. Did he chop that himself? Of course he did. He'd love the predictability, the rhythm of it. I, for one, would love the sweatiness of it. Did he have a wood chopping uniform, or did he do it shirtless...maybe while wearing some low-slung jeans or —*heaven help me*—gray sweatpants?

He pulled inside the single stall—though the effort was pretty much useless now since we were both soaked to the bone—then shut off his engine. He cleared his throat into the suddenly silent space. "I'll show you around, get you something to change into, and then head out."

Oh shit. I hadn't even *thought* of a change of clothes. Or shoes, actually. Or my purse. So I had only what was on my back and my phone that'd been tucked into my pocket when he'd found me. I'd been so dumb struck by Brady's insistence on getting me out of there that I'd left without thinking. So what else was new.

I unbuckled my seat belt and reached for the door handle. "That's awful gentlemanly of you. I didn't think you had it in you."

"And I didn't think you'd actually get in the car unless I hauled you in over my shoulder, so I guess we're both full of surprises."

I stepped out as he did the same and met his gaze over the roof, my head cocked to the side. "Do you feel like the handcuffs were *less* demanding than carrying me over your shoulder would've been?"

Thankfully, he'd had to unlock those cuffs before we could get in the car since crawling over the center console with all his sheriff gear would've been near impossible, but he'd only done so after he'd crowded me into the car, his big body blocking my way and giving me no other choice. He seemed to think I was an idiot, but I wasn't, and he'd made good points. I'd been fine there...until the tree had come down. And by that time, it'd been too late. I hadn't been able to leave anyway, so what else was I going to do but make the most of it?

Brady grunted out some semblance of an answer as he led the way up the couple steps and into his home. He unlocked the door, then held it open for me, gesturing me inside in front of him. I walked past, our skin brushing as I went, and forced down the shiver that worked its way up my spine at his nearness.

My skirt dripped with every step I took, and I cringed at the puddles of water I'd already caused on his wide-planked pine floors. Freezing in place, I pointed to the spot I stood. "Do you want me to just...?"

He stepped up right behind me, so close I could feel the heat coming off his body, and pressed his hand to my lower back, urging me forward. "I live on the ocean, lawbreaker. These floors have seen water."

"Well, color me surprised," I said over my shoulder, the single hall light on in the house casting shadows over Brady's face that only accentuated the harsh lines—his fierce brow, carved cheekbones, and jawline sharp enough to cut glass. The man really was a work of art. "The rigid, rule-following sheriff who likes things just so is okay with a little mess once in a while?"

He stopped just inside the kitchen and stepped around to face me. With gentle, slow movements, he reached up and pulled a tiny twig from my hair before brushing the sodden mass behind my shoulder, the soft brush of his fingers over my collarbone eliciting a trail of goose bumps in its wake. Then he leaned forward so his lips were right next to my ear, his mouth brushing the shell with each word. "When it's warranted, I'm more than okay with it."

My breath got caught in my throat, and I froze. Oh *Jesus*. Was he talking about sex? He was *totally* talking about sex. And I was standing there, completely pantiless and drenched—in all definitions of the word—while this walking, talking wet dream of a man loomed in front of me. So fierce and protective. So solid and sure. So very Brady.

"Noted," I said, planting my feet firmly on the floor so I didn't do something stupid like run away. Or jump into his arms and climb him like a tree.

He pulled back, his gaze dipping to my mouth, and I held my breath, too afraid to burst the bubble of this moment. He swiped his tongue along his lower lip, and I tracked the movement with rapture. Finally, he cleared his throat. "I'll just grab you something to wear and then head—"

His radio crackled to life from where it was secured on his chest, the sound so loud and harsh in the otherwise quiet space, I startled. "Sheriff, can I get an update on your location?"

He maintained eye contact with me as he reached up and pushed a button on the radio. "I'm just getting a few things settled at home, and then I'll be on my way in."

"Afraid you won't. We've got reports of a downed power line on Lincoln, which means you're blocked in. Mother

Nature's spoken, and it looks like she wants you off the clock like you're supposed to be."

Oh shit. This was bad. This was *so* bad. I'd come here thinking I'd have solitude. That I wouldn't be forced to be in Brady's presence and that we'd have a little space from each other to cool down. That usually worked when things heated up between us.

But the problem was, this wasn't the usual form of heat. It wasn't the first time he'd turned me on, no, but something was different tonight. Whether it was the undercurrent of danger, the wrecked and ravaged look he had to him, or simply the fact that my dumb ass hadn't worn panties today, but it was different.

And now, there was no escape.

Brady's jaw ticked as he stared at me, and I wondered if the same things were going through his head that were going through mine—namely, which flat surface to get naked on first.

He held the button on his radio, his eyes locked with mine. "Keep me posted."

"Roger that, Sheriff."

And then there was nothing but silence in the space surrounding us. Though the weight of the tension between us might as well have had a heartbeat of its own, the pulse thrumming so harshly through my body, I swore I could feel it. I wasn't so sure that Brady's and my entire acquaintance thus far hadn't been one big foreplay session. Because as I stood in his house, surrounded by his things and his scent and *him*, I wanted nothing more than to pull his face down to mine and kiss him again.

"Well, it looks like you're stuck with me, Sheriff." I cocked my head to the side and bit my lip, trying to tell myself I did *not* find it attractive as I watched him shed his gear methodically. How that focus would feel directed at me. "How ever will we fill our time?"

CHAPTER ELEVEN

BRADY

WHATEVER CONTROL I'd managed to hold on to snapped in the car the moment Luna said she didn't always wear panties. Her announcement didn't surprise me—this was Luna, after all—but I couldn't stop recalling all our previous encounters and tormenting myself by wondering if they'd been panty days or not. And what was today? Was she standing in my kitchen, wearing only a paper-thin skirt soaked through with rain, absolutely nothing else hiding her pussy from me?

From the heat in her eyes, it was safe to say whatever tether had been holding her back had snapped, too. There was always undeniable chemistry between us—the kind that culminated in fucking or fighting. Trouble was, I wasn't much interested in the latter right now.

Her words hung in the air between us, and I let my gaze caress her body, sweeping over every inch of her. She was soaking wet, probably chilled to the bone. I should be taking her upstairs to shower so she could warm up, but all I could think about was burying my tongue so deep in her pussy she was all I'd taste for days.

I reveled in the feel of her eyes glued to my hands while I unbuttoned my uniform shirt, her gaze drifting lower with each button unsheathed. My voice was too thick, too low, as I said, "Since it looks like we're stuck together, you can either go upstairs and warm up in a shower..."

"Or?" she asked, her gaze still focused on my movements.

I shrugged out of my shirt and tossed it to the side before unbuckling my belt. "Or you can come over here and show me if today is a panty day or not."

Our gazes were locked, the air thick with anticipation and my body strung tight as I waited for her response. With everything I knew about her, I expected retaliation, a smart-mouthed retort that would put me in my place.

What I did not expect was for her to close the scant distance between us in a rush and leap into my arms, the move sending me stumbling back a few steps as I caught her. She wrapped her legs around my waist, delving her fingers into my hair while I gripped her ass—her *bare* ass beneath that skirt—and held her tight as she crashed her lips down on mine.

I groaned into her mouth, taking everything she gave as I spun us so I could set her on the counter and settle in between her spread thighs. Christ, she was just as sweet as I remembered, her tongue sliding against mine as if she was trying to memorize my taste like I was doing with her.

Digging my fingers into the lush curves of her hips, I broke away from her mouth, kissing my way across her jaw to nip on her earlobe. "How many days have you been around me with your pussy bare, lawbreaker?"

She panted, tipping her head to the side and giving me more access as I scraped my teeth down the long column of her neck. "I plead the Fifth."

"All the time?" I asked, shoving the cardigan from her body before sliding my hands under her shirt and removing it from her as well. I groaned when I found her bare beneath it—seemed she didn't just hate panties, but all undergarments—and my mouth watered at the sight of her perfect tits. "Or just specifically when you knew it might piss me off?"

"Believe it or not, Sheriff, not everything is about you," she said with an awful lot of haughtiness for someone who was sitting on my counter, panting, each breath bringing her bare tits closer to my mouth. "I never intended for you to find out my dirty little secret."

"I'm gonna be finding out a lot more of them before the night is through." With that, I lowered my head and engulfed one of her tight peaks in my mouth, sucking deep until she moaned and bowed toward me.

"Fuck," she whispered, threading her fingers through

my hair and working hard to direct me where she wanted me.

Just for that, I bit down on a nipple, hard enough to pull a startled gasp from her lips. "Not yet."

A low whine emanated from her throat, but she took what I gave her as I divided my attention between her breasts, sucking and licking until her nipples were hard and tight, her tits mottled pink from my beard.

I trailed kisses down her body, sucking on the underside of her breast, licking a circle around her belly button, nipping her hip. When I dropped to my knees in front of her, she slipped her fingers into my hair and tugged me closer, her head tipping back on a sigh. "God, yes..."

But that wasn't the game we were playing. Luna was all impulses and whims, but not tonight. I was going to show her how good it could be with a bit of discipline.

I slipped my hand beneath her skirt, sliding it up the inside of her thigh until I reached her center and brushed a featherlight touch over her slit. Never quite giving her what she needed, making her desperate for more. As soon as she arched her hips up, seeking more friction, I landed my fingers on her pussy with a sharp smack.

She gasped, her head jerking to stare down at me, eyes wide. "What the hell?"

Tugging her until her ass was perched at the very edge of the counter, I said, "Stop trying to control this. Your job is to sit there and look pretty while I fuck you with my tongue."

Something sparked deep in her eyes at my words. "You gonna get to that anytime soon? Because I'd really like to have a ride on your cock before you remember sex is messy and you don't do messes, so let's get on with it."

She was right. I absolutely didn't do messes—physically or otherwise. Yet Luna was the biggest mess of all—tumultuous and unpredictable and completely fucking enrapturing—and I was ensnared by her as surely as if I'd been on the receiving end of *her* handcuffs.

I had no idea why she held so much appeal for me. All I knew was if I didn't fuck her out of my system, I wouldn't be able to think straight. Since she'd stepped foot in this town, my thoughts had been consumed by her, like she was the sun and I was just orbiting around her axis. I'd had a month and a half of blue balls, only made bluer after that kiss last week, and I was going to rectify that tonight. It was just sex. And hell, who even knew if it'd be any good between us?

"I'm not going to 'get on with it,'" I said, voice low. "I'm going to fuck you exactly how I want to, and you're going to love every minute of it."

"Oh my God, would you lick my clit already?"

I pinned her with a hard stare. "Shut up and I might."

She pressed her lips together, her hands gripping the edge of the counter as she waited for my next move. Something shifted deep inside me, the notion that this woman, whose impulses usually controlled her, was sitting patiently, quietly waiting for me, was intoxicating like nothing I'd ever experienced.

"Fuck, you're sweet when you obey me."

Her fiery eyes shot to mine, and she opened her mouth on a retort but snapped it shut as soon as my lips and tongue met her skin. I gathered her skirt in my hands, sliding it up her legs and pressing kisses along the revealed skin. Her ankle, her calf, behind her knee...nowhere near where she wanted me, and I was enjoying her squirm.

"Be a good girl and hold this for me," I said, handing her the gathered material of her skirt. "I need to see if your pussy tastes as sweet as the rest of you."

"I could do without the bossing, just FYI," she said through panted breaths, her chest heaving with each inhale and exhale, but she still gripped her skirt and did as I told.

I brushed my nose along her inner thigh, my mouth watering over her scent. Blowing a gust of air directly over her pussy, I bypassed her clit and repeated the motion on her other leg, grinning at her answering whine.

When I finally swept my thumb over her slit, I hummed low in my throat, my cock jerking at how wet she was. "I'm not so sure about that. You're fucking drenched, so it seems your pussy loves my bossing. Now sit back and shut up while I taste what I do to you."

Whatever retort had probably been on the tip of her tongue cut off on a long, low moan when I spread her apart with my thumbs and flattened my tongue against her slit, groaning when her tangy sweetness invaded my senses. Jesus Christ, how could a little demon like her taste like fucking heaven?

I tongued her in long, deep strokes, sucking her into my mouth and soaking up every inch of her pussy. My cock was an angry, throbbing beast in my pants, desperate to get inside her. With my mouth still affixed to her, I held her open with one hand and undid my pants with the other, groaning in relief when my cock sprang free, thick and hard and pulsing with need as I wrapped my hand around and squeezed tight at the base.

"I think I've figured it out," I said against her skin.

"What?" she asked through panting breaths, staring down at me from between her spread thighs.

"Your pussy's soaked up all your sweetness, so that's why you're such a harpy all the time."

"Oh my God." She groaned on a laugh, tossing her head back as her inner thigh muscles fluttered against my ears, and an answering tug in my cock had me gripping myself harder. "I need less talking from you and more licking. Do you need a map to my clit?"

I pulled back, breathing a laugh against her, then very deliberately pressed my thumb exactly where she wanted me and didn't move. "You tell me, lawbreaker. I thought this was going well, but if you'd rather I stop—"

"No! Don't stop. Please don't stop." She shifted her legs, hooking them over my shoulders and trying to work herself against my stationary digit until she finally sagged back with a whine.

Instead of giving her my mouth, I released my cock and slid two fingers inside her, pumping slowly and coating them with her wetness.

"Your tongue, too. Give me your tongue."

I slipped my fingers from her and smacked them hard against her clit, my cock throbbing at her answering yelp. I pressed my hand to her, rubbing over her pussy with a soft caress and gathering her wetness on my fingers and palm. And then I reached down and gripped my cock again, groaning as I stroked her excitement all over my length.

"What're you doing?" she asked, watching me with hooded eyes.

"Exactly what you think I'm doing. I'm so desperate to be inside you, I'm fucking my fist with the proof of just how much you're loving this." I leaned in, grasping my cock with a firm squeeze, and licked a featherlight path up her slit, only the whisper of pressure against her clit.

She moaned loud and long, her hips undulating with every slight pass of my tongue against her. "Please, Brady. Please just—"

"You like knowing that, don't you?" I asked. "Knowing you've got me so worked up, I couldn't even wait to get inside you."

"Yes," she panted, her eyes locked with mine. "But I need more. Give me more. God, please give me more."

I tightened my fist at the base of my cock, holding

firmly as her begging words rushed over me. "Just so we're clear, I'm doing this because I want you to flood my mouth, not because you told me to."

"Yes, yes, fine, whatever. Just please—"

I sucked her clit between my lips and slipped two fingers inside her pussy, as I gripped my cock with my other hand. Fuck, I was as hard as granite and ready to go off like a rocket. I couldn't remember a time I'd ever been so desperate to be inside a woman like I was now. Like I was with *this* woman.

"Oh God. Brady, I'm— Fuck, I'm coming." She released her hold on her skirt and pressed her hands to the back of my head, holding me to her. Eyes glazed, she parted her lips on a moan as she exploded around my fingers...against my tongue. And through it all, she stared down at me with a look of awed rapture while I devoured her whole.

The desire to be inside her was no longer a want. It was a need. A bone-deep yearning to slide into her and feel her clench around me, all while she melted at my touch. Before she could even catch her breath, I stood and shucked off the rest of my clothes. Then I gathered her to me and carried her the few feet to the sliding glass doors that looked out over the ocean.

I set her down on her feet, spun her to face outside, and pressed her against the slider with a palm between her shoulder blades. Her hair was damp, still dripping down the small of her back, her tits bare and pressed to the glass.

She turned her face toward me, but it was too dark to

read her expression. The hall light didn't reach this far, and only pitch blackness greeted us outside. Waves crashed against the shore as rain battered the roof and windows, echoing the harsh urgency thrumming through my veins. I needed inside her, needed to be surrounded by her. Needed to finally quench this thirst I seemed to have for her.

I rucked up her skirt, gathering it in my fists as I slipped my cock between her thighs, sliding it back and forth against her soaked pussy lips. Groaning at how wet she was. How hot. How needy for me.

Lightning flashed outside, showing off her perfect body. Her back was arched, hands pressed to the glass on either side of her head, ass tipped up as she canted her hips toward me, swiveling them as if in search of something. As if in search of *me*.

"Brady..." she sighed, clenching her hands into fists, and I couldn't take it anymore.

"Goddamn, I love it when you say my name." Bending my knees, I gripped my cock, still slick with her arousal, and drove all the way inside her in one deep thrust.

Her answering moan nearly did me in. Fuck. Oh *fuck*. I'd thought about this for weeks, my nights spent imagining all the ways I'd have her. But even with all that fantasizing, I hadn't been prepared for this. Not for her wet heat pulsing around me, or her breathy moans, or her throaty little sighs, or the look in her eyes when the lightning flashed enough to showcase her desire.

I hadn't been prepared for Luna.

"Christ, you feel so fucking good." I pulled out before sinking deep, again and again, the constant friction that'd always been present between us finally exploding in how I fucked into her. Hard and frenzied and as if I'd never get enough.

Because I didn't know if I would.

She reached back and dug her fingers into my ass as I slipped an arm between her and the glass door. I sank one hand between her thighs and fingered her clit while sliding my other hand up between her tits. I wrapped my fingers around her throat, tugging her back for a kiss.

Unlike everything else she tended to do around me, this time, she came without a fight, dropping her head back on my shoulder and opening her mouth for me without hesitancy. I kept my eyes on her as I swept my tongue into her mouth, groaning as the flash of lightning showcased her features. Her eyes were closed, pure bliss written on her face while she took me inside her over and over again. That, paired with the absolute heaven that was her body, nearly did me in.

I fingered her clit faster, stroking circles over the swollen bud as her pussy squeezed me tight. "Fuck," I swore under my breath. Lips to her ear, I said, "Your pussy's a greedy little thing, isn't it? Sucking my cock in so deep. Just begging to come hard all over every one of these nine inches."

"God, yes," she panted out on an exhale, lips parted

and eyes half lidded as she watched me lose my mind over her.

What was this woman doing to me? She turned me inside out, frustrated me to the edge of sanity and smiled while doing it. She infuriated me, exasperated me, and still managed to have a magnetic pull over me like no other.

I needed this to be a one-and-done with her, because I wasn't sure I'd survive otherwise.

"Quit holding back." I gritted my teeth, thrusting into her with wild abandon, the sound of our bodies smacking together mixing with the rumble of thunder and the constant cadence of rain against the windows.

"I'm not," she managed through panting breaths, her head resting on my shoulder as her fingernails dug sharp crescents into my ass.

"You *are*. I worked up this pussy, made you dripping wet. This orgasm is mine. I earned every bit of it, and I want to feel it around my cock. Now, give it to me." I slapped her clit, tightened my fingers around her throat, and sank my teeth into the space where her shoulder met her neck.

Her body went tense even as my fingers strummed her clit in a blur, my cock thrusting so deep, I wasn't sure where she ended and I began. Her pussy fluttered, tightening impossibly until she let out a long moan, the sound reverberating against my hand, and pulsed around me, coming with my name on her lips.

"That's my good girl. Just like that. *Fuck*." No longer

able to hold myself back, I turned my face into her neck and sank deep with a groan. I spilled myself inside her, her pussy rippling around me through her aftershocks and pulling every ounce of my orgasm from me.

We stood there for long moments, only our panting breaths between us, her body still pressed against mine. All the while, I ignored how much I loved it. Told myself it was just because I hadn't had sex in a while. It was the circumstance, not the woman, that'd turned me inside out.

It wasn't until I pulled out of her, my cock slipping from the warm, wet heaven between her legs, that I realized my mistake.

I'd fucked her without a condom. Ridden her bare and then come inside her without an ounce of protection between us. Worse, without even a whisper of a thought about it.

I swore under my breath, scrubbing a hand over my face. I didn't make mistakes. I was regimented for a reason, had lived my life that way for a long damn time. And I'd certainly never lost myself so much in a woman that the mere thought of a condom hadn't even entered my mind. I'd never once had sex without one. But all I'd been able to think about was being inside her.

If I didn't watch myself, all my carefully curated control would slip right through her fingers, and she'd look at me with a sparkle in her eye as it flowed through her hand.

What I really needed to do was run far away from this clusterfuck of a woman, remind myself of all the reasons this was a bad idea. A long-winded list of why this should've been a one-and-done. Why she wasn't worth the challenges she brought with her. Why I had no business involving myself with her at all.

But all I could think about was how soon I could be inside her again.

CHAPTER TWELVE

LUNA

IT WAS STILL DARK when I tiptoed my way down the hallway to Brady's bedroom. After our fuckfest downstairs, he'd shown me to the bathroom for a shower—without him—and then deposited me in his guest room—also without him. With a mumbled goodnight, he'd left me in there with barely a glance in my direction.

And. Well. That just wouldn't do.

Brady had surprised me, and considering the rigidness of his personality, I'd assumed that was impossible. But hours ago when we'd gotten here and found out we'd be stuck together, it was like a light had switched on in him. And I, for one, wasn't complaining. I'd thought sex with him would be boring and methodical. I'd never been more wrong about anything in my life, and I'd been wrong about a lot.

His bedroom door was ajar, and I took that as invitation and crept inside. Rain still pounded against the house, the random flashes of lightning exposing the space and showing me a blink of Brady in all his glory. He lay on one side of his king bed, sound asleep on his back, the sheet pooled around his waist showcasing his bare chest. And my *God* what a chest it was. He was broad and solid, with a soft dusting of dark hair that led straight down to the ridges of muscles on his abdomen I wanted to spend hours tracing. I'd barely even gotten to touch him during our earlier tryst, and I was none too happy about it.

The cut lines of his Adonis belt disappeared into the band of his boxer briefs, and I cursed them and the fact that I hadn't gotten an up close and personal look at what he was packing. But considering my pussy still ached hours post-coitus, I could guess.

Three steps into the room, the floor creaked under my weight, and Brady lifted his head from the pillow, eyes snapping open and landing immediately on me. I froze, unsure whether I should continue toward him or turn on my heel and head back to the guest room and the too-big bed I'd felt lost in.

"What's wrong?" he asked, instantly on alert even though his tone was low and gravelly from sleep. And sweet *Lord*, the things it did to all my good parts. When had his voice stopped irritating me and started turning me on?

"Your guest room is very nice, but I'm afraid it's just not for me."

DEFIANT HEART

He stared at me for a long moment, then dropped his head back to the pillow and sighed heavily. "Couldn't your critique of my home wait? It's two a.m."

I shrugged, the neckline of Brady's T-shirt slipping off one shoulder. "Yeah, and I've just been lying there this whole time, wide awake, because the bed's too big."

"The bed's too big," he repeated, his tone flat.

"Yes." I stepped toward him, very aware of my bare legs and the lack of, well, anything beneath his shirt, and sidled up to his side of the bed. A bed, by the way, that came up to my waist. I'd need a fucking ladder just to climb into it. "You know I'm used to sleeping on a twin mattress, right? In a tiny little van? My body doesn't know what to do with all that open space."

"And you're in here because..."

"Well, you're an overgrown jackass, so I figured you probably hogged the bed, too. No doubt you'd shove me to the edge and I'd feel right at home and fall fast asleep."

In the flash of lightning that lit the room, I swore I saw his lips twitch into a smile, but then it was gone as he studied me for several long heartbeats, his gaze drifting over my body beneath his oversized shirt, and my nipples pebbled at his scrutiny. Finally, he said, "Is this your way of getting me to fuck you again?"

Ignoring my body's response to him and his words, I breathed out a laugh and pressed my hand to his chest, leaning down until our lips nearly touched. "No, Sheriff.

129

You destroyed my pussy earlier, so I'll need a bit of a break from your monster cock before we try that again."

Though, who knew if there'd be an again. He'd shut down so quickly after coming inside me—without a condom, by the way, which had necessitated a terse conversation about test records and birth control (covered on both counts, thank God)—that I assumed it would be a resounding no. But from the way he stared up at me, the flash of lightning through the room showcasing the hunger and heat in his eyes, well...now I wasn't so sure.

I also wasn't so sure I'd say no to round two.

Being with Brady was a bad idea, without question. But I'd never been one to shy away from bad ideas. In fact, I tended to run toward them at full speed without thought of consequences.

Still looming over him, I lifted my head a few inches until I could no longer feel his breath on my lips. "Come on, grump. I'm tired and want some sleep. Just let me snuggle for a while. My feet aren't *that* cold, and I won't make a peep, promise. You can go back to hating me in the morning."

One minute, he was challenging me to a staring war, and the next, he wrapped his thick arm around me and hauled me onto his bed, pulling me straight over top of him and settling me on his other side. He kept his arm around me, tucking me in close and pulling the covers over me as if it was second nature. His hand landed on my ass, tugging me against his side, and then he froze, his fingers flexing against the material hiding all my bits.

He tipped his head down to me, his breath ghosting over my hair. "You came in here with a bare pussy, but you're still trying to tell me you weren't aiming to get fucked, lawbreaker?"

I shifted against him, laying my head on his steel wall of a chest. My nipples tightened into hard points thanks to the heat radiating off him. Or it could've been how he palmed my ass like it was his hand's designated resting spot. Or the fact that he was half naked with nothing more than a flimsy piece of cotton keeping me from seeing all his goods. Could be anything, really.

"That's exactly what I'm telling you," I said, hand flat on his stomach. And if I petted that stomach, admiring the ridges of muscles and the thin trail of hair that disappeared into his boxer briefs, well. No one could prove it. "You shoved a T-shirt at me, grunted, and then fled like your dick was on fire. If you wanted my bottom half covered, you should've given me a pair of boxers, too."

He grunted, still palming my ass like a basketball. "Thought you said you wouldn't make a peep if I let you in here."

"Quit asking me questions, and I'll be quiet," I said against his chest, still trying to get comfortable. I snuggled in deeper, pressing my ice-cold feet to his shins and grinning at his answering hiss.

"Not too cold, my ass," he mumbled under his breath.

"I don't know how the feet of one of Satan's minions can be so fucking frigid."

"It's a lot warmer in hell. I'm not used to the climate change yet." I turned my head into his chest, inhaling against his skin and closing my eyes as I took his scent deep into my lungs. It was...warm. Just warmth and salty ocean air. It was Brady, and I couldn't deny how much I loved it.

"Did you just sniff me?"

"Did you bring me out to your murder lair? It's awful quiet out here."

"Keep talking, and you'll find out," he said, his words muffled against my hair.

"Just wondering why you live out here and not at the resort."

"And I'm wondering why I agreed to let you in my bed and why I thought you were telling the truth when you said you wouldn't make a peep."

"That's not an answer."

His heavy exhalation gusted over my head, his chest rising and falling under my cheek. "Just couldn't live there anymore. Not after—" He cut himself off and cleared his throat. "Well, not after. I needed a space of my own."

It took everything in me not to ask, "*After what*?" and demand details about his cryptic answer. But I wasn't in a position to demand anything from Brady. That didn't stop my curiosity over the man, though.

I shifted and adjusted against him, trying to find a

comfortable position. All the while, his hand never left my ass, the one anchor to him as I moved this way and that. In one of my adjustments, I brought my knee up to hook over his legs, inadvertently brushing against his dick. His hand tightened on my ass, but otherwise, he didn't acknowledge it.

So I did it again, a little firmer this time as I slid my hand down his stomach to rest just above the waistband of his boxers. He was hard, his cock thick beneath my thigh, and I wanted another ride, tender pussy be damned.

"You're playing a dangerous game, lawbreaker," he said lowly, his lips brushing my forehead with each word.

I crawled my fingers across his stomach, dragging them back and forth along his waistband. "Those are the best kinds to play."

His whole body was stiff. Poised. Ready to strike at any second. I'd wondered what it'd be like to have all that control unleashed on me in the heat of passion. Wondered if it'd be boring and rigid. Unremarkable. But while he'd still held the control earlier despite my fighting him tooth and nail, it'd been a completely different kind of control. One filled with passion and dominance that I was all too sure not many people saw. And the thought that I'd brought it out in him was a shot of ecstasy thrumming through my veins.

Finally, his chest rumbled beneath my cheek as he spoke. "Thought you said you were too sore."

I did. I was. But...was I *really*? I was pretty sure my

vagina would forgive me for using and abusing it like this, especially when I was faced with the specimen that was Brady and the tool he wielded like a goddamn pro.

Just once more. Once more wouldn't be awful, right? Once more, where I could really get a good look at him... spend some quality one-on-one time, just me and his dick. We'd both get our rocks off, and then things between us would calm down. All that animosity would be alleviated, and we could be...friends?

"I lied." I slipped my leg farther over his, pulling myself up to straddle his hips.

He brought his hands to my outer thighs, his fingers slipping under the fabric of his T-shirt as he stared up at me, his cock already straining against the confines of his boxers. "Thinking about doing something, then?"

"Maybe."

The man was ripped, no doubt about that, and I felt like a wisp of a woman next to him. His body radiated power, and it was a natural high to know I could bring him to his knees. I brushed my hands over his pecs and the light dusting of hair there, sliding them up to his shoulders, then down his biceps, loving how firm and solid he was beneath me. Totally unshakable. But I'd shaken him hours ago, hadn't I? Could I do it again?

"Just so we're clear..." he said, slipping his hands under the shirt I wore and lifting it up and over my head, baring me to him completely. He tossed it to the floor as he reached up and cupped one of my breasts, thumbing a nipple and tugging until I gasped. "Just because you're on top doesn't mean you're in charge."

"I don't know." I rocked over his cock, sliding my pussy against him as I braced myself on his arms. "This feels a little like I'm in charge."

"Does it?" He gripped my waist, hauling me up his body as if I weighed nothing until I hovered over his face, my pussy inches from his mouth. "'Cause I promise you're not. Now, put your hands on the headboard and ride my tongue like a good girl. Gotta make sure this pussy is nice and soaked if you want to take my cock again."

Jesus, this man had a way with words that shot straight to my clit, the traitor throbbing with anticipation and desire, knowing what awaited it if only I'd succumb. So I did what any girl who was facing the choice between being in charge or getting eaten out by Brady would do—I placed my hands on the headboard like I was told and sat on his face.

His mouth was open and waiting for me, his tongue seeking me immediately, and I tossed my head back on a moan at the first delicious touch. I'd been so wrong when I'd thought he surely wouldn't do this because it was messy. No, Brady ate pussy like a man on death row being served his last meal. He sucked and nibbled, licked and swirled until I was a writhing, panting mess above him. Wrapping his arms around my legs, he gripped my thighs from below and devoured me.

I ground against him, using the headboard for leverage

as I rocked back and forth on his face, each flash of lightning through the room illuminating us for a tiny blink of time. But no matter how far apart those flashes came, Brady's eyes never strayed from my face. He stared up at me from between my spread thighs as he licked my clit and fucked me with his tongue, his gaze speaking of want and desire and so many promises of what tonight would bring.

When he sucked me hard between his lips and gently scraped his teeth against my clit, I came. Back bowing, I shuddered and shook over him, my thighs trembling, hands still clinging to the headboard as if they alone could anchor me when the feelings he wrung out of me sent me flying.

Aftershocks still racked my body when Brady shifted and suddenly flipped me so I lay on my back, my head at the foot of the bed as he loomed over me.

"Wait," I said breathlessly, body still shaking through my release. "I wanted to have a chat with your dick."

Breathing out a laugh, he shook his head. "Later."

He braced his hands on the backs of my thighs and spread me wide, tucking my knees up to my chest. And then, without any buildup or easing the way for the monster between his legs, he drove deep inside me, stealing the air straight from my lungs.

"Fuck. *Fuck.*" He stared down, dividing his gaze between my face and where he disappeared inside me. His eyes were dark and angry, like he was pissed we were this perfect together in bed. "You shouldn't feel this good."

"Back atcha," I attempted to say, though it came out as more of a moan than anything.

I didn't know if it was the angle he hit, the look of blissful agony on his face, or the fact that he'd thrust into me before I'd even come down from my first orgasm, but he sent me flying again. Immediately. My body was in a tailspin as wave after wave of euphoria crashed over me.

"Oh God," I choked out, hands gripping his forearms as he fucked me straight through my orgasm, my pussy clenching hard around him.

"Still think you're the one in charge, pretty girl?" His head hung between his shoulders, and his fingers dug so deep into my thighs, I was sure I'd have bruises there in the morning, but I didn't care. Didn't care a single bit when he was making me feel this good. "I'm the one working this pussy up, making you come so hard you see stars. Remember that."

I didn't have it in me to argue with him. Could barely manage single syllables at this point. All I could do was hold on while he fucked me like a man possessed. Like he wanted to burrow so deep inside me, he'd never come out. Like he never wanted it to end.

"Once with you wasn't enough," he said, his hands still braced low on the backs of my thighs, thumbs running up and down my pussy lips as he thrust into me. "You think two'll be the magic number? Or am I still gonna be craving your pussy when I wake up in the morning and can still taste you on my tongue?"

Before I could respond—with what, I had no idea—he pinched my clit, rolling it between his thumb and forefinger, and I jerked my legs closed, the stimulation too much after coming twice in a row. "I don't— I can't—"

"Yes, you can," he gritted out through clenched teeth. "Spread those legs for me, lawbreaker, and hold on. You're gonna be a good girl and give me another one. I want to feel your pussy squeezing me one more time."

"No, I can't." I shook my head even while doing as he said. I gripped behind my knees, holding my legs tight to my chest as Brady fucked me with a single-minded focus. It didn't matter, though. I'd never, ever come more than twice from sex. And twice was a stretch. Okay, once was a stretch, but that was what B.O.B. was for, right? "You won't be able to make me come again."

He stared down at me, shoulders tight and jaw clenched, looking like an angry avenging angel—or a demon sent straight from hell to tempt me. "Watch me."

Still rolling my clit between his fingers and pumping his cock into me with slow, shallow thrusts, he palmed my lower stomach, his fingers stretching hip to hip. Then he pressed down on his next thrust, and I swore the entire fucking world could've exploded around me and I wouldn't have cared.

My eyes widened, mouth dropping open on a gasp when he stroked the spot inside me. And then kept stroking it, over and over again, never losing his rhythm. This man I'd fought with for weeks and had fucked only twice had found—and exploited—what I'd only ever been able to reach with a specially designed vibrator.

"*Oh shit*," I breathed, lips parted as I held my legs to my chest, spread open and waiting for him to send me where I needed to be. I split my gaze between his face, drawn in concentration, and where his cock disappeared inside me, its girth stretching me to a beautiful, pain-laced pleasure.

He let out a self-satisfied hum as my body responded to him, and he continued the slow, exquisite torture, playing my body like it was an instrument he'd studied for years. Never speeding his thrusts or increasing the pressure, even though I begged. And I did. I begged and pleaded, babbled incoherently as my orgasm built slowly inside until I could do nothing but wait for the wave to pull me under.

"Christ, you're squeezing me so fucking tight. You're gonna soak my cock, aren't you, pretty girl? Gonna come all over me and prove I'm the one in charge of this pussy."

Light burst behind my closed lids as a riptide swept me away, and I came on a choked sob, my heartbeat snuffing out every other sound in the room. The pleasure was blinding, exploding through me as my pussy pulsed with every wave that crashed over my body until I was a sated, boneless heap on the bed.

"That's my good girl." Brady's groans filled my ears as soon as my heartbeat receded, and he dropped down, covering my body with his. He slipped his arm beneath me, sliding his hand up to grip my nape as he drove into me with slow, deep thrusts, his lips resting against mine. "You look so fucking beautiful coming all over my cock."

God help me, but when he said things like that, it made me forget that we didn't work. Didn't make sense. That what we had was pure, carnal lust, plain and simple.

But when he held me tight and covered my mouth with his, filling me so slow and sweet, it was hard to remember all the reasons we weren't a match. Hard to remember why we wouldn't work. When he captured my lower lip between his, brushed his tongue against mine even as he settled deep and spilled himself inside me, he made it so easy to forget.

Through panting breaths, he kissed the corner of my mouth, my jaw, behind my ear, before pressing his face into the crook of my neck to catch his breath. And there, so soft I wasn't sure I was supposed to hear, he mumbled, "Twice isn't going to be nearly enough."

CHAPTER THIRTEEN

LUNA

THE FAINT SOUND of a ringing phone woke me, my body curled around a pillow that smelled an awful lot like Brady as if it were a raft in the middle of the ocean. I buried my face in the cotton cloud and inhaled deeply as images of last night—both times—crashed through me. My body heated all over, recalling exactly what Brady had been able to evoke in me and shuddering at the thought. After less than twenty-four hours, he already knew how to turn my brain into mush and turn my body into a live wire, so I'd hate to see what would happen if we spent any more naked playtime together.

Okay, that was a lie.

I wouldn't hate to see it. In fact, I was damn curious. Would it only get better the more we learned, growing hotter and hotter until I burned from it, or would it fizzle out and fade away to nothing when he'd uncovered every bit of me and decided he didn't like the raw, undiluted version of me, like every other relationship I'd ever had?

Though, truth be told, none of my other relationships had ever started like this. With a pull so deep, it felt like an actual tug under my skin. A connection so undeniable, I ached to be near him, even if just to bicker.

I reached around blindly, hoping to come in contact with a very warm, very hard body and see if he was up for round three, but ultimately came up empty. Lifting my head from the pillow, I glanced around the space I hadn't gotten a good look at last night to find I was alone.

Sunlight streamed through the partially closed curtains, brightening Brady's bedroom. It was clean and fairly barren—just this gigantic, ridiculously comfortable bed, a dresser, and a nightstand made of dark wood...none of which held any personal effects, though the faint scent of Brady still hung in the air. How long ago had he left, and why hadn't he woken me up to kick me out when he'd gone?

The quiet of the space was interrupted by the sound of my phone ringing from down the hall, and I realized that was what had woken me in the first place. I shoved the fluffy dark-blue duvet off myself, catapulted off the bed to the floor, and picked up Brady's discarded T-shirt before slipping it on. I padded down the hall to the guest room and picked up my phone, wincing as I found an incoming

FaceTime call from my mom. I hadn't stopped to glance at myself in a mirror, but I probably looked like a woman who'd been fucked within an inch of her life last night. But, well, it wasn't like she thought I was a virgin.

I smoothed my hair back and accepted the call, holding the phone out in front of me as I plopped down on the guest bed.

Before I could say a word, Mom said, "*Well*..." with far too much excitement, her eyes pinging all over the screen as she no doubt catalogued every hair that was out of place and whatever the state of my face was. "I'm glad to see the *storm* didn't ravish you last night."

I breathed out a laugh and rolled my eyes. "Morning, Mom."

"Mhmm...morning, indeed." She smirked as she propped her elbow on the table, the ever-present stack of bracelets jangling on her wrist as she rested her chin in her hand. Her eyes, the same blue-hazel as mine, stared back at me with interest. "I saw a replay of Mabel's Live this morning and the damage the storm had already done last night, so I figured I'd give you a call. Where are you, anyway? That doesn't look like the inside of your van."

Well, this was going to be fun.

"It's not. Brady came by last night in the middle of it and brought me to his place because a big old tree was blocking my path out."

As usual, Mom totally ignored the part about me being

trapped and possibly in danger and instead focused on the man. She hummed, eyes sparkling. "Brady, huh? That's weird... I could've sworn that was the name of the sheriff. You know...the one who keeps arresting you."

"*Kept*. He hasn't arrested me in at least a week."

Mom laughed outright at that. "I take it you worked out all your differences, then?"

Flashes of last night blinked through my mind—how intense it'd been. Heated and passionate and full of whatever crazy chemistry constantly zinged between us—and I had to squash down the memories, willing my cheeks not to redden. "Hardly. We're still at each other's throats."

Mom grinned. "Well, that can be very fun, too. You know how much your father and I are opposites..."

"Okay, Mom, that's enough," I said with barely restrained laughter.

My mom was my best friend and someone who didn't know the meaning of personal boundaries. That meant I knew far more about her sex life than I ever, *ever* wanted to, and she thought it was perfectly normal to ship me a "cool new vibrator" she'd heard about because "very few men actually know what they're doing, and sometimes you just need a helping hand." She'd raised me under the notion that sex was never a dirty word. It was just another beautiful thing in life, like dancing in the rain or swimming in the ocean, and she had no qualms slipping it casually into any and all conversations. Had no qualms grilling me about the status of my sex life, either.

Mom laughed. "I'm just saying, a little animosity never hurt anyone in the bedroom."

"Who said anything about the bedroom?"

"Oh, my sweet girl. I know you don't think I'm that naive. You've been on birth control since you were sixteen."

I heaved out a sigh. "Let's talk about something else, shall we?"

Mom smirked, her eyes sparkling, but she let me change the subject. "Fine. Since you're...*enjoying yourself*... with the sheriff, can I assume things have smoothed out on the development front?"

The mention of it made my stomach clench with unease. The complications of trying to put a stop to something that was very obviously at odds with what Brady and his family were trying to accomplish muddied my convictions. I didn't want to hurt them, and that was the problem. It was why I didn't get involved with men who didn't share my views or my passion for activism, and I certainly didn't get involved with those on the other side of the law. It was just begging for trouble.

And yet there I was, in Brady's home, wearing his shirt, smelling like him, and still tender from how he'd taken me last night, practically on my knees for it.

I blew out a heavy sigh. "Not even a little. A motion for discovery has been filed—Brady fast-tracked it in exchange for me staying out of their hair while a journalist sniffs around the resort—so it's just a waiting game right now."

"And what's your plan when the findings come back?"

Plan? I didn't do plans. I flew by the seat of my pants, took things as they came, so I'd figure that out when the time arrived.

"Pretty sure you know the answer to that."

"Right, no plan. Well, your dad's looking into it, too, after he saw that Live where you chained yourself to the tree. Good work, sweetie, but we both thought you caved awfully quick. Since when is food enough to get you to give in?"

I huffed, knowing she was right. I'd fucked up that morning by not packing my essentials, but I wasn't one to look back in regret. Whatever happened, happened, and I moved on from it. "It wasn't just the food. It was raining, too, so they were going to have to pack it in for the day anyway." Then I recalled the deliciousness that was the Luna Special and sighed. "Plus, you've never had this omelet."

"Hmm... Maybe I will. Your dad and I were just talking about taking a weekend trip somewhere, so why not there?"

"Sure." I shrugged, knowing damn well my parents weren't coming up here. My mom's whims were wilder than mine, and she rarely, if ever, followed through on what she said she would. I'd learned that lesson at a very young age. Until I saw their car pulling up in front of me, I'd assume she was blowing smoke up my ass.

"Maybe then I could meet this mysterious sheriff. Where is he now, by the way? And, more importantly, can I assume he's the reason for that beard burn on your neck?"

"Oh my God, Mom." I groaned, tugging up the neckline of Brady's shirt, as if that would do anything now.

"What? I'm just happy to know my baby has an active, fulfilling sex life. It *is* fulfilling, isn't it? There's nothing worse than a dead fish in the sack. Does he know how to, you know, *get you there*? If not, there's nothing wrong with moving things along yourself. That vibrator I sent you would be perfect for that. It stimulates oral sex, and—"

"Oh Jesus," I muttered under my breath. "Mom, please. I'm begging you. It's too early for your brand of girl talk. Where's Dad? At least his presence would keep you from interrogating me about my sex life."

"You know it wouldn't. He'd just stalk off in a huff, muttering how he didn't want to hear it."

"As a parent should."

She harrumphed. "Well, you don't have to worry about him overhearing. He's at the office, working on an important case. And anyway, I'm not interrogating you. I just want to know where the man who very clearly ravished you is at seven thirty in the morning."

"I don't know, actually..." I paused, listening for clues from the rest of the house, but it was silent, the air still. Without looking around, I knew I was alone. And why my heart sank at that realization, I had no idea. It wasn't like

Brady owed me anything. After all, he'd already given me several of the most intense orgasms of my life. I wasn't expecting breakfast in bed.

"Hmm...leaving you after...*rescuing*"—she said rescuing like one would say *defiling*—"you last night. What do we think about that?"

"It's fine. He's a sheriff. I'm sure he had sheriffy things to do after the storm. There was a downed power line, and the town's probably a mess, so he's—"

"Yes, yes, very busy, I'm sure." She sniffed. "Well, if you're not upset, I guess I don't need to be either."

"I'm not, and you don't, I promise."

After another few minutes in which she tried and failed to get me to detail last night's activities and then a promise to keep her updated on both the shopping center situation and whatever was going on with Brady, we said our goodbyes. I hung up, starfishing on the bed for a second, before I dragged myself out of the room and headed to the bathroom.

I'd been in too much of a stupor last night when Brady had handcuffed us together that I hadn't grabbed anything from my van, which meant I had my phone and the clothes on my back and that was it. After taking care of my business, I washed up and then dug through the drawers, grateful but unsurprised to find a few unopened toothbrushes inside.

After brushing my teeth, I headed into the hallway,

intent on snooping. If Brady was okay leaving me in his home unattended, I had no problem nosing around. Still wearing only his T-shirt, I made my way through his house, taking my time and studying it now that it wasn't pitch black and my thoughts weren't consumed by horniness.

His home was as tidy as I'd expected, with thick-planked pine floors throughout, the walls painted a soft, muted gray. Upstairs held only the master bedroom and en suite bathroom—with a multi-headed shower I'd love to take for a spin—and the equally unappointed guest bedroom and bathroom.

Maybe the main floor would give me more of a glimpse into the elusive man that was Brady McKenzie. I slipped downstairs, stopping at the base of the steps to take in the main floor. The kitchen, dining room, and living room all flowed into one gigantic space, three sets of glass sliders on the far wall showcasing a view of the ocean.

To my right was the living room with an old-fashioned woodstove, plus a couch and matching oversized chair, a bookcase, and a TV. A small dining table for four separated the living area and kitchen, which was simple with white cabinets and stainless-steel appliances—all of it spotless.

I strode over to the center slider along the back wall, pressing my palms to the glass as I stared outside—I'd already left prints of both the hand and boob variety thanks to last night, so what were a couple more? "Holy shit," I breathed.

I stood in a near replica of the stance he'd put me in the night before, but then I hadn't been able to see anything but darkness beyond the glass. Today, though, I took in the beauty that was his backyard. A deck stretched along the entire length of the house. Steps led down to a small grassy area cut off by a winding path made of sand with a direct line straight to the ocean. His backyard looked like a freaking postcard with the sun shining and illuminating a glittering path over the water. As I stared out at it, a warm sort of peace settled over me that I'd only ever experienced from the back of my van.

What would it be like to wake up to this every day? To sit out on the porch and soak in the sun, meditating to the lullaby of the ocean?

Knowing I could get lost in that view for hours and unsure of how much alone time I had in the house, I dragged myself away and poked around, hoping for a clue into this man I knew so little about. But the whole house felt...cold. It was a beautiful piece of property, tucked away from everything, if the darkness surrounding us as we'd driven up last night was any indication, but it lacked heart. The place needed some rugs, a few paintings, and would it kill him to display some knickknacks? Hell, he didn't even have any junk mail lying around.

The only remotely personal thing I came across was a grouping of photos clustered on his bookcase—that held, naturally, a plethora of true crime novels. There were three pictures in varying sizes. The smallest was a young Brady, with two missing front teeth, standing next to a man who had to be his father. His dad smiled at the camera, but Brady's attention was solely on his father, staring up at him as he held a small fish.

Next to it was an image of him and his siblings—all of whom I'd met, with the exception of Levi, though he wasn't hard to pick out since he was the only one I didn't recognize. The picture looked to have been taken maybe ten years ago. I could make out everyone, but there was a softness to their faces they no longer carried. They stood around the sign for Starlight Cove Resort, and though they smiled, there was no denying the overwhelming sadness in each of their eyes.

The last and largest picture of the bunch showed a beautiful woman with dark-auburn hair, pale-green eyes the exact shade of Brady's, and a smile that lifted straight off the image. She stood in front of a large sailboat, six kids all clustered around her. They ranged in age from maybe twelve—Brady—to Addison, who looked to be around three or four, sitting propped on her mom's hip, everyone beaming at the camera.

The difference between the older pictures from when Brady was a child and the one from his adult years was staggering. Where the older ones were full of happiness and life, the more recent one felt...empty.

I had no idea what caused the shift, but that wasn't

what troubled me. Nope, it was the fact that I wanted to know in the first place. I knew better than to get in deep with someone like this—with anyone at all. And yet I couldn't stop myself from wanting to dig deep and uncover all his secrets.

CHAPTER FOURTEEN

BRADY

LAST NIGHT HADN'T GONE REMOTELY how I'd planned. Though that seemed to be par for the course when it came to the tornado that was Luna. She'd dropped into Starlight Cove out of nowhere, ravaged everything in her path, stirring up things that were better left untouched, and I was worried nothing would ever be the same in her wake.

I'd lain there for a solid hour after I'd fucked her in my bed, holding her while she'd fallen almost immediately into sleep and wondering how the hell I'd ended up there. With a beautiful woman I had no business getting involved with curled into my body and snoring softly against my chest, her skin still smelling faintly of me.

Eventually, I'd fallen asleep, only to wake a couple hours later to my alarm. I'd slipped out from under Luna, who'd barely stirred, and left her without a backward glance—because who the fuck knew what I'd do if I turned around and caught a glimpse of her lying naked in my bed? Sure as hell not me. I'd already proven that I didn't know what the hell to do when it came to her. So I'd showered in the guest bathroom, staying as far away from her as I could, before heading to the station to deal with the clusterfuck that would be today since the downed power line blocking me in had been taken care of.

The arts festival was scheduled to start this evening, but the town was a mess thanks to last night's storm. Fallen branches and various debris littered the streets, so cleanup was in order. Thankfully, that would keep me from thinking about Luna. And last night. And early this morning.

Unfortunately, that plan went about as well as any plan where she was concerned. By midmorning, even with everything needing my attention, I'd given up on avoiding thoughts of her. I'd figured it was a lost cause when I found myself in the café, searching the menu for something disgusting for her to eat, before I'd even realized what was happening.

And now, I drove toward my house to greet the woman who drove me out of my mind—with frustration and need in equal parts—a green smoothie resting safely in the cupholder. It wasn't the ass-water Beck fed her, but it was the closest thing I could get without heading out to the resort.

I had no idea why I'd gotten her anything at all. Or why I was taking this mini-break, considering the state of the town and the amount of work still needed to get things squared away before the festival. *And* considering the fact that I didn't do breaks. I ate at my desk or in my patrol car, radio always at the ready. And yet, here I was. Delivering breakfast to the only woman besides my sister who'd ever been in my home.

I parked in my garage and grabbed her smoothie before heading inside, unsure and a little apprehensive of what I'd find. I didn't figure she'd been able to do much damage in the few short hours I'd been gone, but then, I'd made the mistake of underestimating her at first meeting, and I didn't intend to do that again.

I set my keys on the counter, the sound startling her as she spun to face me from where she stood in the living room. She wore the T-shirt I'd given her last night, show-casing far too much bare skin, and I couldn't deny what the sight did to me. Or how much I liked seeing her in my clothes and in my space.

She held a picture frame in her hand as she scanned me from head to toe, her brows lifting when her gaze zeroed in on the cup I held. "Morning, Sheriff. That for me?"

I grunted and set it on the kitchen counter. "I'm sure as hell not going to drink it."

She placed the photo down and strolled toward me, all long legs and tight nipples that winked at me through the plain white shirt. Why the hell had I given her *that* and not, say, a parka?

I inhaled when she stepped close, biting back a groan when I realized she still smelled like me... And ignoring just how much I loved it.

She lifted the cup and sniffed, her eyes locked on mine, one brow raised.

"What the hell are you doing?" I asked.

"Making sure you didn't poison it."

I rolled my eyes, grabbed the smoothie, and took a deep pull from the straw, preparing myself for the onslaught of trash. But I was pleasantly surprised when the liquid hit my tongue. It might not have had all the disgusting ingredients she preferred, but it was infinitely better than the shit Beck was slinging. "Poison doesn't smell. It'd sort of defeat the purpose, don't you think? Maybe you could try that on me instead of irritating me to death."

"Where would the fun be in that? And I knew it wasn't poisoned." She grinned as she lifted herself up onto the counter, and I tried to ignore the long expanse of her legs and the fact that she still wasn't wearing any fucking panties. "I just figured you could use some fruits and veggies in your diet. Done with your shift already?"

I fisted my hands, ignoring the incessant itch to slide them up her thighs, tug her to the edge of the counter, and lick up all her sweetness, just like I'd done in this spot the night before. "Not for a while."

She cocked her head to the side, lips pulling steadily from the straw, and I steadfastly ignored what the sight did to my cock. "Then why are you here?"

That was a damn good question and one I didn't have an answer for. One I didn't want to dig too deeply into, either.

"Figured you'd burn down my house in retaliation if I didn't feed you. I know what kind of irrational things you do when you're hangry."

"Way to save that, Sheriff." She reached out, running a soft hand down my chest. "For a second there, I thought you were being nice."

I grunted, glancing over to the bookcase she'd been standing in front of when I arrived home. "Have fun snooping?"

Her grin widened around the straw, her eyes dancing, but she didn't respond.

"Find anything good?"

"No, actually." She brushed against my uniform pants with every swing of her legs, her blue-painted toes sweeping against my thighs, and since fucking when did *toes* make me hard? "I was kind of hoping I'd find a sex dungeon or a box of kinky toys."

I cleared my throat, forcing myself away from thoughts of dragging Luna into a sex dungeon or using a box of kinky toys on her. "Sorry to disappoint," I said, my throat full of gravel, cock hard as steel.

"You didn't." Her eyes sparkled. "I *had* wondered if

you'd been spawned from a demon, so it was good to confirm you came from actual humans and weren't hatched somewhere." She tipped her head in the direction of the photo she'd been holding when I'd walked in. The one of my mom and us kids taken more than twenty years ago.

"How do you know I still wasn't?"

"You look too much like your mom." She reached up, brushing her fingers down my temple, and I had to force myself not to lean into her touch. "The eyes are undeniable."

I knew that fact all too well. I saw a poor facsimile of her every time I looked in the mirror, and I hated it. "My dad used to tell me that."

She rested her hand on my shoulder, cocking her head to the side. "Used to?"

The last thing I wanted to do was talk about the shitty, fucked-up relationship I had with my father. Not when she was in front of me, her legs parted just enough for my hips to fit between them. "We don't speak anymore."

She made a gruff sound of commiseration in her throat. "And your mom?"

"She's dead."

In the almost ten years that she'd been gone, the words had gotten easier to say. They were just words after all. They didn't encompass the pain and grief my siblings and I had gone through in the days and months following her death. Didn't encapsulate what it was like to have to shove everything aside—emotions included—just to make sure things stayed on track. Didn't even begin to cover how difficult it was to keep moving through life when your guiding force was suddenly gone.

"Oh, Brady," she said, her voice soft and fingers softer as she trailed them down my chest. "I'm so sorry."

I didn't know if it was the look in her eyes, the tenor of her voice, or the feel of her fingers against me, but I'd never before wanted to fall into someone's embrace as much as I did in that moment, with this woman. But down that path led only madness—or poor decisions, as it were —and I wasn't in the market for either.

"Thanks," I said flatly.

Without another word, I stepped away and grabbed her clothes from the laundry room where I'd hung them last night. I thrust them out at her, avoiding eye contact. "Get dressed. I'm heading to the resort to check for damage. We can swing by your van so you can grab some things."

"Don't you mean so you can drop me off? I have to lead a class for that journalist and give her a massage."

"Fine, but you're coming back here tonight. I can't get anyone out to clear the tree today. Not with the festival starting."

After what'd happened between us last night, would she sleep in the guest room like I'd intended, or would she sneak her fine ass into my bed again? Maybe have that talk with my dick she mentioned in her orgasm stupor... I clenched my teeth, forcing the thoughts out of my head. She shouldn't be here in my home. I shouldn't *want* her here. But I couldn't deny anymore that I did. She drove me crazy, but she brought a lightness to my days that had been missing for far too long, and I'd begun to crave her when she wasn't near.

She pursed her lips as she grabbed her clothes from me. "We'll see."

And then she hopped down from the counter, whipped the T-shirt over her head until she was standing in my kitchen bare-ass naked, and proceeded to get dressed. Slowly.

I'd felt every inch of her last night, had been inside her with my tongue and my fingers and my cock, but it'd been too dark to see her in all her glory. And her glory was fucking stunning. Small tits, a waist that dipped in at her sides with a subtle flare on her lower stomach, and the lush, supple curves of her hips, thighs, and ass. Curves I was sure I'd never get sick of.

"Oh, don't look so stunned, Sheriff. You've seen my tits before and quite literally had your face in my pussy." She pulled on her clothes while I stood there, still—and hard —as granite.

Once she was dressed, she braced a hand on my chest and stood on her tiptoes, tugging me by the back of the neck until she could press her lips to my ear. "By the way, could you still taste me this morning? 'Cause I sure as hell could still feel you."

Then, with a small, soft kiss against my jaw, she stepped back, grabbed her phone and the half-drunk smoothie, and waited for me at the side door, a twinkle in her eye that said she knew exactly the state of my dick right now. And she liked it.

TEN MINUTES LATER, I pulled up to the same spot I'd parked last night, only this time, everything was different. My heart seized in my chest, the organ feeling like it was caving in on itself, as I stared at the scene in front of me. Holy shit. *Holy shit.* A tree, smaller but no less intimidating than the one originally blocking the path, had fallen. Directly on top of Luna's van.

"Oh my God," she said, hands covering her mouth, eyes wide as she stared out the windshield.

Oh my *fucking* God was more like it. My palms were sweaty, my pulse thrumming wildly, and I felt like I couldn't catch my breath. Jesus *Christ*, what would've happened if I hadn't come out to get her last night? If I'd ignored the tug in my gut to check on her and instead had just gone straight home? She would've been trapped inside there with no way out.

Or worse, crushed beneath the wreckage.

I reached up, rubbing the deep ache in the middle of my chest, needing another minute or twenty before my heart would settle back into its normal rhythm and this pit in my stomach would close. But Luna didn't give a single fuck about that as she unbuckled her seat belt and fumbled with the door handle. She also didn't give a single fuck that she didn't have any shoes on. She tore out of the car, dead set on sprinting across the debris-ridden forest floor and cutting the shit out of her feet in the process.

Having her dashing out was like paddles to my chest, jolting me out of my stupor, and I jumped out of the car and caught up to her in front of the hood. Without letting her take another step, I hooked an arm around her waist and tugged her back to me, just taking a second to feel her body against mine. To breathe her in and reassure myself she was fine. She was okay. She was alive and safe and *fine*.

Then, before she could question what the hell I was doing, I swung her into my arms, bracing one around her back and the other beneath her knees, and strode toward the van.

"Hey! What—"

"You're barefoot."

She rolled her eyes. "I'll be fine, grump. Believe it or not, I *have* walked around barefoot once or twice in my thirty-one years."

Whoever let this woman loose in the world was a menace to society. She was a magnet for trouble and needed a goddamn keeper, and it looked as if I'd been volunteered for the job.

"Yeah, well, if you get cut, I'll just have to administer

first aid, and I have more important things to worry about today."

She smiled, clearly seeing through my bullshit answer, and reached up to wrap her arms around my neck. "Be careful, Sheriff. All this worrying about me might go to my head."

"I don't know what you're talking about," I grumbled under my breath.

Her answering laugh was halfhearted at best as she focused all of her attention on her van. The closer we got, the tighter my chest grew, until it felt like a vise was squeezing the life out of me. Branches draped over the entire expanse from the back end to the hood, the tree trunk resting right smack in the middle. Right where she would've been sleeping.

Jesus fucking Christ. She would've been in there. Would've been under that.

I didn't know how long I stood there, staring at the wreckage, Luna clutched in my arms as I held her too tightly against me, until her words finally registered.

"It's okay. I'm okay," she said, over and over, as she played with the hair at my nape and ran her fingers along my neck, her touch light and reassuring even as I nearly crushed her to me. "I need to get inside."

No. I didn't want to set her down, let alone allow her to go into the death trap she called a van.

"I'll go," I said, my voice coming out gritty like sandpaper. "Tell me what you need."

She huffed out a laugh and shook her head. "Brady. I can't open the back or side door, which leaves the driver's side, and there's no way you're going to fit through the passway. *I* barely fit. Plus, it's not like the tree is going to suddenly fall *more*. It's as far down as it can go."

Her words made sense, but that didn't stop the overwhelming urge I had to clutch her to my chest, turn around, and run her straight back to my house and lock her inside. Irrational. Completely fucking irrational, and she'd think I'd lost my mind if I uttered a single word of it. So instead, I just stood frozen, staring at what could've been a catastrophic accident.

"C'mon, grump. Set me down." She rubbed her hand on my chest, directly over my heart, the repetitive motion soothing something deep inside me. "The quicker I grab my stuff, the quicker we can leave."

"Fine," I finally grumbled. "But I'm checking it out first."

I carried her over to the driver's side, found a clear patch of grass, and set her on her feet. Then I reached for the door handle, my jaw ticking when it opened immediately.

"Oh, don't give me that look," she said with an eye roll. "We've got bigger things to worry about, don't you think? Besides, you didn't exactly give me time to grab my keys last night."

"Or panties," I mumbled under my breath as I slid into the driver's seat.

"Or panties," she repeated with a cheeky grin. "Plus, I don't think I need to worry about someone stealing my van. What with the gigantic tree pinning it down and all."

"I'm not worried about someone stealing your fucking van," I bit out, my temper getting the better of me as I glanced into the back to see the damage. The roof was caved in, a huge dent directly above her bed. Directly where she would've been lying during the storm. *Christ*, my chest hurt.

I slid out of the van, not wanting to let her go in there but knowing I could either be here when she did it and make sure she stayed safe, or I could keep her from it, only to have her sneak back after I'd headed into town. Yeah, she was a slippery little thing, but I'd learned her tricks in the month and a half she'd been here.

After I stepped off to the side and made room for her to go in, she rolled her eyes. "If someone stealing my van isn't what has your balls all tied up in knots, what is it, then?"

She didn't wait for an answer before she disappeared through the small pass-through, my heart in my throat the entire time. Good, because I didn't have an answer to give her. Not a sane one, anyway. What could I tell her? That the thought of her getting hurt made me fucking crazy? That the idea that she'd been out here, for weeks, without anything other than a rock collection to protect her made me sick for no good reason, and imagining her out here during the storm made me want to throw up my breakfast? Yeah, no. I'd keep that shit to myself.

A few minutes later, after I'd circled the van and catalogued the destruction, Luna crawled out from the back, large bag in hand and shoes on her feet. She made a huge production of shutting her door before holding up the key fob in between us and locking the van with a beep. "Happy?"

Was she doing that shit on purpose just to get a rise out of me, or did she truly not understand I was more worried about her being *in* it when her doors weren't locked and any troublemakers or criminals having complete access to her than whatever trinkets she kept that petty thieves would steal? Didn't matter, because I wasn't happy about *any* of this. Not her out here in her van, not her staying in my home, not her in Starlight Cove.

She'd gotten under my skin and made me feel things I hadn't felt...ever. I wasn't even this protective over Addison. My brothers and I would go to the ends of the earth to keep her safe, but it was wholly different from the thrum in my veins I felt for Luna.

"Hardly," I answered, leading us back toward my patrol car, keeping close to her to make sure she didn't stumble.

I shouldn't have been worried, though, because Luna strode through the forest like it owed her something. Like her safe passage was guaranteed and something as silly as a branch or exposed root wouldn't dare to get in her way.

It wasn't until we were settled back in the patrol car, making our way toward the main inn, that Luna broke the silence. "Thank you."

I snapped my gaze to her, only to find her eyes already trained on me. Eyebrows lifted, I said, "I must've heard you wrong. What was that?"

She rolled her eyes, but a smile tugged at the corner of her lips. "I said thank you. If you hadn't been an idiot and cuffed yourself to me last night, forcing me to leave, I'd have been inside the van when that tree fell."

I inhaled sharply, images of her trapped inside with no way out flashing through my mind, and I gripped the steering wheel tighter.

"And I probably would've peed myself if that happened, and we both know I wasn't wearing panties, so it would've been a big ol' mess." She inhaled deeply, then released the breath on a long, slow exhale. "So, thanks. I guess following protocol isn't always bad."

I huffed out a laugh, not finding this remotely funny. "Nothing about last night was protocol."

Her eyes stayed locked on me, her gaze like a brand against my skin, heating me up from the outside in. "Then why'd you do it?"

Wasn't that the million-dollar question? It was easy to say I had no idea what made me do it. No idea why I'd forced her hand last night just to keep her safe. But I was afraid I *did* know why, and it was worse than not knowing at all.

Instead of answering, I just clenched my jaw in response, leaving her question hanging in the air between us.

CHAPTER FIFTEEN

LUNA

AFTER SLOWLY DRIVING through the preserve, avoiding all the fallen branches and debris, Brady pulled up in front of the main inn. I turned to him, intent to tell him thanks for the ride, but he was already out of the car and walking around to my side before I could utter a word. He opened my door, one brow cocked when I didn't scramble out immediately.

I rolled my eyes and stepped out of the car, tossing my bag over my shoulder. "Believe it or not, Sheriff, some people actually use *words* to tell people what they're thinking rather than just facial expressions and grunts."

Still silent, he locked his eyes with mine as he reached out and slid my overnight tote off my shoulder, then he stalked toward the entrance, purple floral bag gripped in his hand.

"You didn't need to walk me to the door," I said as I

followed behind him. "I don't think I'll come across anything that will cause me harm in fifteen feet."

"I need to talk to Aiden and Addison."

Oh. Well. That made a lot more sense than what had been going through my mind since we'd pulled up to the scene of the crime—namely, that he couldn't let me out of his sight because he was as shaken up as I was over finding my van pinned under a tree. But no. People didn't fret over me like that. I was Luna—the girl with nine lives who always seemed to land on her feet. I couldn't be knocked down or out, so why bother worrying?

Brady held the door open for me, and we stepped inside, his fingers just a whisper against the small of my back, and I shivered at the touch. Aiden glanced up from the computer he was focused on behind the check-in desk, brows lifting as he split a glance between Brady and me.

"Hey," Brady said, setting my bag down on the counter.

Aiden's brows lifted even farther. "Hey…"

If Brady noticed the underlying question in his brother's tone, he didn't show it.

"How're things here?" Brady asked. "I didn't see too much damage to the property when we drove through."

Before Aiden could respond, Addison came around a corner and answered without looking up from her phone. "Not awful. We've got one downed tree by Cottage Fifteen and a bunch of stray branches, but it's nothing Ford can't take care of."

"Good, because I won't be able to help for a bit," Brady said. "Too much shit in town to worry about."

"Speaking of, how's it looking for the festival tonight?" Addison pocketed her phone and slipped around the counter, shoving Aiden aside as only a baby sister could. "We've gotta set up our booth. Beck's got the menu all ready, and we're going to do a raffle for a free weekend stay."

"Thought we weren't in the market for giving away free cottages," Brady said dryly.

A smile swept over Addison's mouth, and she beamed at him. "We are when there's promo involved, and this will be great content for our social media." She leaned forward, elbow on the counter as she rested her chin in her hand, eyes sparkling as she split a glance between Brady and me. "Besides, it seems things worked out okay…"

"What thing—" Aiden started to ask, but Brady cut in before he could even get the sentence out.

"You should be fine to set up in a few hours. The power's back on. It's still a mess, but a cleanup crew will be starting in—" Brady looked at his watch, then headed for the door "—fifteen minutes. I'll be back after my shift." He pinned me with a look, one that damn near had me melting on the spot. "Stay out of trouble." And then, without another word or a backward glance, he blew through the door.

"He seems especially grumpy today," Addison said, staring after her brother.

He did, indeed. One would think all the sex would've knocked that stick loose, but apparently I was going to need to work a little harder on that endeavor. He was probably mad because he was going to be stuck with me for a bit while I figured out what the hell to do with my van and how to get it fixed. I'd have to check for auto body shops in town later this afternoon and get that squared away. Maybe I could figure out a rental in the meantime...

Addison furrowed her brows. "And, wait... Did he say he was coming back here after his shift? Why?"

"Because a tree decided to take a nap on top of my van," I said. "And because your brother's a Neanderthal."

"Oh my God!" She clasped her hands over her mouth and dashed around the counter, looking me over from head to toe. "Are you all right? Were you in the van when it happened? Or did he pick you up last night?"

"Jesus," Aiden said under his breath, his attention on his laptop. "Give the woman some space, Addison."

I laughed, patting her on the shoulder. "Yes, no, and yes. He dragged me away last night before it got too bad. And I mean that almost literally."

She cringed. "Sorry about that. It was sort of my idea."

My brows shot up. "It was your idea that he handcuff us together?"

"He *what*?"

I waved a hand through the air. "Whatever. Never mind. He's a caveman, I'm safe, it's all fine." I grabbed my bag and hefted it over my shoulder as I headed farther into the inn.

"Harper's gonna be here shortly, and I want to make sure everything's set up. We still need to sell this, right?"

"Right," Addison said, eyes pleading. "So if you could—"

Aiden cut her off. "Not do or say anything at all, that'd be great."

Addison reached over the counter, palmed her brother's face, and gave it a shove. "Don't listen to the idiot. What he means is if you could just...you know...not—"

I held up my hand and grinned. "I got it. Be a little less me. Focus on extolling all the wonderful aspects of the resort and Starlight Cove, and mum on the whole deforestation and greedy corporations taking over small-town living. Roger that."

I gave her and Aiden a thumbs-up, then headed to the parlor. Harper's one-on-one yoga class was scheduled to start in thirty minutes, but I wanted to make sure the space was perfect. Start off on the right foot and all that. Since it was a little too cool—and a little too debris-strewn—this morning to comfortably be outside for our practice, I was going to have to bring the outside in.

Twenty minutes later, I'd changed out of yesterday's rainwear and set up two yoga mats in front of the wall of windows, a couple of them open to let in the sea breeze and the sounds of the waves crashing against the shore. A diffuser misted lavender and lemongrass essential oils into the air, and several jar candles flickered around the space.

Having no other guests at the resort was a problem, for sure, but in this instance, it only added to the peaceful ambiance.

Starlight Cove Resort really was the perfect location for this type of activity. With its sprawling oceanside beachfront, it was a haven of tranquility. But even if it wasn't possible to be outside, I could bring enough of it inside to make it all still feel connected.

I sat on my mat in Sukhasana, facing the floor-to-ceiling windows with an unobstructed view of the ocean, and forced myself to be present in the moment. I inhaled the tranquility and peace of the space, exhaling any fear or anxiety my body still held over finding a huge tree crushing my home. Yes, it was *just* a van, but that van had been where I'd lived every day for the past three years, and finding it demolished had been heartbreaking.

I continued on for several breaths, but my pulse still fluttered, my nerves frayed. God, if I hadn't gone with Brady last night—if he hadn't shown up in the first place—I would've been in there when the tree had fallen. I'd talked a big game last night, telling him I was a grown woman who could take care of herself, but I'd just been being stupid.

Of course I could take care of myself—I'd been doing it nearly my whole life—but I couldn't deny how unexpectedly nice it was to have someone actually looking out for me. Someone checking in on me. Someone making sure I was safe and not taking for granted that I had everything figured out.

And for that person to be Brady...well, that was a twist I hadn't seen coming.

WHILE SPENDING the day doing what I loved helped keep my mind off my current situation, it had never really left me completely. Harper had been a fantastic student, not overly familiar with most poses but eager to learn more about the practice. And the massage had mostly been low groans of appreciation—from her, obviously—and very little talking, so I took that as a good sign. I'd tried to get her to spill the tea on what the status of the article was or which direction her editors were leaning, but she wouldn't say a word.

Still, during the quiet pockets of time during the massage, and now after, my thoughts had been consumed entirely by my ruined van. My *home*. My whole life was in that 6 x 10 space, and I didn't know where I went from here.

My first order of business would probably be to get it towed and get an estimate on damages to figure out whether or not it was totaled. With Harper tucked back at her cottage, I strolled toward the main inn and called the auto body shop in town, figuring now was as good a time as any.

"Frank's Auto Body," a man answered, his voice low and rough, like he'd smoked a pack a day for the past fifty years.

"Hi. This is Luna Lancaster, calling about—"

"Sure, sure, Luna. Has anything changed with your van?"

Brows furrowed, I opened and closed my mouth a few times, having no idea how to respond to that odd question. "Well...kind of? Considering there's a giant tree crushing it."

He laughed, a deep, husky sound that reverberated through the line. "Besides that. Sheriff McKenzie already called and got you all squared away. I've got your number, so I'll call you with an estimate once we can get out there and have it towed back here so I can see what we're working with."

"Brady called you?"

"Sure did. Several hours ago, in fact."

If he'd called that long ago, that meant he'd done it shortly after he'd dropped me off at the main inn. Had he mentioned that before he'd left that morning? Definitely not. There was no way I'd forgotten that, even in my haze. And I certainly hadn't asked him to do so—I'd just figured out where to call fifteen minutes ago.

Which meant he'd just...done it. So I wouldn't have to worry about it.

Warmth bloomed in my chest, thinking of the big, bad,

gruff sheriff taking it upon himself to make the call and take this off my plate. Just because.

"Luna? You still there? Damn phones are always—"

"Yes, sorry. I'm here. That, um, that sounds good. Thanks."

"Happy to help. Like I told the sheriff, depending on what we find, you might be looking at quite a while before the damage is repaired. Sheriff McKenzie wasn't sure what your schedule was like or when you planned to leave town, but this is gonna be quite a speed bump if you're hoping to get out quick."

The sheriff wasn't the only one who didn't know that small detail. No matter where I'd gone these past three years, I never had a plan for where I went or how long I'd stay. Either a freelance gig brought me to a town, or I simply rolled up when someplace felt right, got settled, and then left when the wanderlust struck once again. But I'd been in Starlight Cove for a month and a half, and the urge to up and flee hadn't hit me even once.

This town—and the people in it—had grown on me, settling deep into my soul. And now...I wasn't sure I *wanted* to leave. At the very least, I wanted to stay to see through what I'd started with the motion for discovery on that piece of land. I might've only been here for a short time, but I loved this town enough to want to make sure a corporation didn't snuff out the beauty of Starlight Cove. I'd seen enough to know bringing in a national chain would only crush every single locally owned store along their beautiful Main Street. Businesses would fold. Families would suffer. And I didn't want to see that happen to the people I'd grown to care for.

I didn't want to see that happen to Brady and his family, which left me in quite a tight spot, considering our goals were conflicting.

But after? I had no idea. It'd always been my plan to leave, and I hadn't been quiet about that. Hell, it could've been the whole reason Brady felt secure enough to start something with me in the first place—because he knew it wouldn't last. That I wouldn't last.

I'd never ached for anything permanent in my life, but as I ended the call, I couldn't ignore the sharp tug in my heart that felt an awful lot like yearning for permanence. And not just any permanence, but permanence here. With him.

Slipping my phone into my pocket, I stepped through the door to the main inn. I didn't make it two steps inside before Addison snapped her head up from where she stood behind the counter next to Aiden.

"How'd it go?" she asked with not a little bit of apprehension in her voice.

Shaking off my feelings of unease and grateful for the distraction, I shot her and Aiden a wide grin. "Great! We made plans for tomorrow morning at the Williamsons' property. She's going to join me so she can get a front-row seat as I chain myself up and get the scoop straight from the source."

Addison reared back, her mouth dropping open on a gasp, as Aiden stared at me with wide eyes.

I didn't even make it ten seconds into the bit before I cracked up, laughing at their horrified expressions. "Oh my God, you should see your faces."

Aiden scowled, resembling Brady more with every furrow etched into his brow, and Addison actually stomped her foot, her hands fisted at her sides. "That wasn't funny."

"Oh, come on." I giggled. "It was a little funny."

"What was a little funny?" Brady asked as he stepped inside. His gaze swept over me from head to toe in a move that almost seemed perfunctory if not for the careful way he studied me as if checking that I was all in one piece, or how my nipples peaked at his perusal.

"Luna woke up this morning and chose violence, apparently," Addison said, glaring at me.

"I don't know what that means. She hit you? Why, what'd you do?"

"No, she didn't hit me, you idiot." Addison rolled her eyes. "And for the love, Brady, would it kill you to at least *scroll* social media once in a while? You're not eighty."

"I'm also not interested. Why don't you harass Aiden about that?"

Aiden leaned a hip against the counter, crossing his arms over his chest. "It's cute that you think she doesn't."

Addison rolled her eyes. "Yeah, yeah, I'm an equal opportunity harasser when it comes to my dumb brothers.

Speaking of harassing, why are you out of your uniform? You're not thinking of going to the festival, are you?" she asked incredulously.

I slid my eyes over to Brady in time to see him shrug. "Don't know," was all he said. Enlightening.

Addison smirked and split her gaze between Brady and me, her eyes alight with interest. "Well, well, well, that's certainly new."

"What is?" I asked.

"Brady doesn't usually—"

"Why are you still here?" Brady interrupted. "Who's helping Beck at the festival?"

"Point taken, you big oaf. And Ford's with him." She shut her laptop and tucked it away before stepping out from behind the counter. "I'm heading over there now. Aiden, you good?"

He waved her off without a word, and she headed out. Then, after I'd gathered my bag—which Brady immediately took from my hand—we did the same.

Once outside, Brady walked straight to the passenger's door and opened it for me, setting my bag inside. But before I could slip in, he pinned me to the car with his body, one hand gripping my hip and the other cupping the back of my neck. With his thumb under my jaw, he tipped my head back before brushing a featherlight touch over my pulse.

"You good?" he asked, his eyes searching mine. As if it

was more than a superficial question. As if he truly wanted to know the answer.

So I told him the truth. "I was a little shaky this morning, but I'm okay now."

He hummed low in his throat, darting his eyes all over my face, probably checking to make sure I was telling the truth. He must've concluded I was because he lowered his head and kissed me. Soft and slow until he slid his tongue against mine and turned the kiss into something hungry and deep. Like he was reacquainting himself with my taste. Like he wanted to drown in it.

Finally, he pulled back, leaving me panting for breath and wondering if it'd really be that bad to jump his bones right out here in the open, even with his brother so close. But before I could, he shot me a look that said he knew what I was thinking as he helped me into the car and then shut the door behind me.

"Rude," I said to myself as I got buckled in, waiting for Brady to slip into his seat.

Once inside the car, he said, "I've gotta drop something off quick, and then we can go to the festival if you want."

I tucked my leg beneath me and turned toward him as he drove us through the resort, a grin spreading across my lips. "Was that your way of asking me out on a date, Sheriff?"

He grunted, the sound low and deep and highly unamused. "Yes or no, lawbreaker."

"That depends. Will there be funnel cakes at this festival of yours?"

"I didn't realize funnel cakes were organic."

"Oh, shut up and answer the question."

"Of course there will. We're not monsters."

I gasped loudly as I reached out and gripped his forearm, loving the flex of muscle beneath my fingers. "Holy shit, was that a joke?"

His scowl deepened, and he kept his eyes glued out the windshield as he parked in front of one of the cottages. "You've got until I get back in the car to make your choice, or I'm making it for you."

With that, he slipped out, grabbing two paper grocery bags from the back seat before heading toward Cottage Thirteen and depositing them in front of the door. The cottage looked like all the others at the resort—well-worn, but well loved, with a plethora of flowers in the pots bracketing the porch steps and nothing inside to hint at any life within. Without so much as a knock, Brady spun around and strode straight back to the car.

Once he'd slid into his seat, I asked, "What was that?"

"Groceries."

"For who?"

"What's your answer?"

"What?"

"The festival. Yes or no."

I blew out a sigh, knowing he'd told me all he intended

to about his mysterious delivery. "Yes, obviously. This'll be my first Starlight Cove festival, so you better make it good."

He slid his gaze to mine, leveling me with heated eyes. "I think we both know I can make it good."

I shifted in my seat, still hot and bothered thanks to that kiss and grateful I'd put on panties when I'd changed into leggings and an off-the-shoulder sweater that was thick enough to hide the state of my nipples. The more layers between Brady and my ravenous body, the better.

As he drove us toward Main Street, I studied him in the light of the setting sun. He'd changed out of his uniform before he'd picked me up at the resort and now wore a long-sleeved olive-green Henley that did amazing things for his eyes—not to mention his body—and worn, faded jeans that looked buttery soft. So very different from the buttoned-up sheriff I normally saw.

"Do you usually bring a change of clothes to the station?" I asked.

"What?" He spared me a glance out of the corner of his eye before returning his attention to the road to find us a parking spot. "No, why?"

I shrugged, a smile tipping up the corner of my lips. That meant he'd known he'd be taking me to the festival tonight—or hoping to, anyway. Otherwise, he wouldn't have had the jeans and shirt with him. Had he been busy cleaning up the town while also trying to figure out how to ask me out on a date, while *also* making sure my van was being looked at? The thought loosed a flurry of butterflies in my stomach, the swoop and flip of my insides a new, if welcome, sensation.

I didn't get heart-fluttery for men. Didn't feel like a shaken-up champagne bottle, ready to burst with one little look. At least not until Brady.

With a grin, I said, "No reason. Thank you, by the way."

"Don't thank me yet. What if you hate it?"

"Not about the festival. Thanks for calling Frank about my van." I reached out and rested my hand on his forearm. "That was really sweet of you to do that for me."

He shrugged, clearly uncomfortable with my gratitude. "It was no big deal."

Maybe not to him, but to me, it was. I'd been making my own appointments since I was thirteen—doctors, dentists, therapists... You name it, I did it. Had even perfected my mom voice to call myself out of school when need be. His doing this for me was such a tiny thing— probably inconsequential to most—but sometimes those were what hit the hardest.

Showing someone you cared wasn't always about surprise trips to Paris or spa getaways or a brand-new car with a bow on it. Sometimes it was about filling up their gas tank or making sure their favorite coffee never ran out. Sometimes it was dragging someone out of a thunderstorm, or hanging their only clothes to dry, or bringing them breakfast you'd never eat yourself, or making an appointment so they didn't have to.

I had no idea how to convey that to him—or even if I

should—so I stayed quiet as he parked us within walking distance of the festivities. Main Street had been shut down, with blockades on each end to stop traffic. The hodge-podge of old storefronts were the backdrop to the numerous white tents set up along either side of the street, strings of white lights draped between them to light the path. The vendors ranged from various food booths to crafts to paintings and handmade goods, all from Starlight Cove and the surrounding areas. A local band had set up in the large gazebo at the center of the park, and people crowded around it, dancing in the grass despite the fact that the band was only a couple steps up from awful.

"You wanna dance?" I asked, tipping my head in that direction.

"I honestly can't think of anything I want to do less," he said but still reached for my hand and clasped our fingers together.

I laughed, leaning into his side as we walked away from the gazebo and toward the tents. "You sure know how to make a girl feel special, don't you?"

I'd meant it as a joke, considering his complete lack of tact, but no matter my teasing tone, it didn't make it any less true. He'd made *me* feel special, and I wasn't even sure he realized he was doing it.

Initially, I hadn't known how to take Brady. Hadn't known what to do with someone so utterly focused on me. I'd never doubted that my parents loved me, but they'd encouraged and cultivated my independence as a young child, and that hadn't wavered. They'd always assumed that I could take care of myself. That they didn't need to worry about me. And though I *could* take care of myself, sometimes it was nice to know I had someone looking after me. Concerning themselves over my well-being as if my being okay wasn't a foregone conclusion.

It felt nice to be looked after when I'd spent a lifetime looking after myself.

While there was no denying Brady and I had started this relationship as adversaries, somewhere along the way, things had changed between us. Shifted in a way I hadn't expected.

I'd stopped seeing him as just the pain-in-the-ass sheriff intent on throwing up every roadblock known to man to stop me from causing trouble in his little town. Instead, I'd begun to see him as just Brady—the man who dragged me away from precarious situations, gave me a place to stay when I didn't have one, let me crawl into his bed for a snuggle, and took me to a festival when it was very clearly not something he was normally interested in.

Whether he'd intended to or not, he'd allowed me a glimpse of the heart that lay beneath that rugged exterior, the single driving force in everything he did. And I didn't know what it meant that I was ravenous to uncover even more.

CHAPTER SIXTEEN

BRADY

I DIDN'T DO FESTIVALS. Hell, I didn't do yoga or skip work to find toilet water smoothies and bring them to a girl I couldn't stop thinking about, either, yet here we were.

Starlight Cove had more festivals than were strictly necessary, and they were definitely more in Addison's and Beck's wheelhouses than they were in mine. I'd spent plenty of time at them throughout my life, but I hadn't been to one in something other than an official capacity in years. It...wasn't awful. Though I knew that had more to do with the fact that I was here with Luna than anything else. Seeing it through her eyes, her excitement and curiosity lighting her up from the inside out, was an experience in and of itself.

Normally, I spent Friday nights at home in front of the TV with a beer—or if it had been a particularly shitty week, a glass of bourbon—decompressing. Fridays were always when I dropped groceries off at Cottage Thirteen, which was, granted, not the smartest way for me to end the week. And yet I did it every Friday, without fail. Even though no one expected me to—hell, no one even knew I did—and I didn't have to continue, it might as well have been a blood oath for the sanctity I put on it. And every week, without fail, it put me in a shitty mood.

But tonight, being here with Luna, my chest wasn't tight, memories didn't have me in a choke hold, and the overwhelming sense of failure didn't swamp me like usual. Whatever magic thrummed through this woman's veins, she'd obviously managed to imbue a bit in me, too, just by being near me.

Luna reached up with the hand that wasn't still clasped in mine and brushed her thumb between my brows. "What's with the scowl? Are you grumpy because they're not making our delicious funnel cake fast enough?"

We stood off to the side, waiting for Mrs. Engles, my former third grade teacher and now blissful retiree who made funnel cakes and cotton candy as a hobby, to give Luna her one and only requirement for attending the festival.

"Just thinking about all the tickets I could write."

Luna laughed, her eyes lighting up in a way that dropped an unpinned grenade straight into the center of my chest. "Then it's a good thing you're off duty. Unless, of course, you have your fun police badge with you? People *do* seem to be having an awfully good time here, and I'm sure that's against some sort of regulation."

That startled a chuckle out of me, and she seemed just as surprised by it. Christ, the mouth on this woman made me want to stuff her with a ball gag and kiss her all at once.

I released her hand and wrapped an arm around her waist, cupping her ass as I tugged her in close. I didn't care that we were out in public. Didn't even care that no one here had ever seen me with a woman other than my sister. I needed Luna close to me. After knowing what could've happened last night had she not come home with me, I had this overwhelming urge to have my hands on her constantly, and I had to force myself not to just strap her on like a backpack and go about my day.

I lowered my mouth so my lips brushed the shell of her ear. "Keep it up, lawbreaker, and see what I do to that mouth of yours when we get home."

Instead of snapping back with a snarky reply, she tipped her head back to stare up at me. She rested her hands on my chest, her lip caught between her teeth and a glint in her eye that spelled trouble. "Promise?"

Fuuuck. The things she did to me. I didn't think it was possible to be so aggravated and aroused simultaneously, yet Luna was all about challenging me. She'd been doing it since the moment she'd stepped foot in this town and hadn't stopped for a second. The woman drove me out of my mind, questioned me at every step. And somehow, in the weeks since she'd shown up in Starlight Cove, I'd actually begun to enjoy it. To crave it.

"Here you go, honey!" Mrs. Engles called, sliding a fried mass of definitely not organic powdered-sugar-covered dough toward us.

With a kiss to the underside of my jaw, Luna pushed away from me and turned her beaming smile on the older woman. "Thank you! It looks *so* good."

"These are normally extra," Mrs. Engles said as she gathered up containers from a few different bins beneath the white folding table serving as a counter. "But I haven't seen the sheriff out of his uniform at one of these festivals in *years*, and I bet we have you to thank for that. Did Brady tell you I had the absolute pleasure of having him in my third-grade class?"

Luna's eyes were filled with interest and amusement as she glanced back at me over her shoulder. "He did not, but I'd *love* to hear some stories. Was he a hall monitor back then?"

Mrs. Engles laughed. "Heavens, no. He was a lot more easygoing when he was younger, but, of course, that's to be expected. What with the hardships his family has faced in recent years." She tutted, lips turned down at the corners. "Such a shame what they've been put through."

Luna shot a worried gaze in my direction, the concern etched across her face hitting a nerve deep in my chest. I didn't want to talk about it—here, of all places—and I certainly didn't want to open myself up to old wounds. But

I couldn't look away from the worry I saw in her eyes, wanted to reassure her I was okay. I was certain in that moment that if she asked me to reach into my chest, rip out my heart, and hand it to her, I would've.

"Sheriff," Mrs. Engles said, pulling me away from Luna's magnetizing stare, "didn't I send you to the principal's office for putting a whoopie cushion on my seat?"

My lips twitched. "More than once."

Mrs. Engles laughed heartily, slapping a hand down on the table, and Luna finally dragged her worried gaze away from mine and back to the older woman. "You were such a hoot as a boy. Anyway, Luna, just think of these as a little thank-you." She slid the stack of three small containers across the table, the translucent cups showcasing what appeared to be chocolate, caramel, and strawberry toppings for the funnel cake.

Luna smiled. "That's very sweet. Thank you. Though I don't know that I deserve the appreciation for getting him here. I'm not even sure what I did to entice him out of his hermit hole."

"I'm sure your mere presence was enough."

Luna threw her head back on a laugh, like those words were the most hilarious thing she'd ever heard. She didn't realize Mrs. Engles was being serious. She also didn't realize my former teacher wasn't wrong.

"Pretty sure that's not it," Luna said once her giggles had died down.

"Well, whatever you're doing, it's working. Keep it up for however long you're here."

And that was the real punch in the gut, wasn't it? All of this—the good, the bad, and the ugly where Luna was concerned—was just temporary. Starlight Cove wasn't a permanent destination on her map of adventures. It was just a stopover. And when the hell had that fact gone from being what I wanted to being what I wanted to avoid?

With a wave at Mrs. Engles, Luna dragged me over to an empty picnic table, strings of white lights surrounding the area and providing a soft glow now that the sun had set. I straddled the bench as she sat next to me, her legs beneath the table and sugar feast spread out in front of her. And then she dug in.

"Oh my God," she said around a moan, her eyes fluttering closed as she licked chocolate sauce from her thumb, my cock twitching at the sight. "I know these are *so* bad for you, but they're so delicious. Here, you've gotta try a bite."

Before I could protest, she held the fried dough against my lips, brows rising when I didn't open immediately. "Do you have to be so obstinate about absolutely *everything*? Just open your damn mouth, grump, and eat this deliciousness before it drips all over me."

Jesus, the thoughts those words conjured in my mind— of her hovering over my mouth, her pussy dripping for me as I licked up every drop—made me a little slow to respond. Just when she rolled her eyes and started to pull her hand away, I reached up and gripped her wrist, tugging it back to me and taking the proffered treat from her fingers. Then I sucked each digit into my mouth, swirling my tongue and licking them clean of the mess, our eyes locked the entire time.

She shifted in her seat, her lips parting as she watched me, gaze growing heated as I swirled my tongue around the tip of her finger. "Good?" she asked, her voice thick.

How long did we have to stay at this stupid thing? I'd wanted to bring her here because I knew she'd like it, but now, all I wanted was to get her back to my place, toss her on my bed, and fuck her until my name was the only sound coming from her lips.

"Not the best thing I've had in my mouth in the past twenty-four hours."

She breathed out a surprised laugh and shook her head. "Look at you, Sheriff. First, a joke in the car, and now, an innuendo-laced play on words? Careful, I think I'm rubbing off on you."

I thought she was, too, and I didn't hate it.

When she pulled another chunk off the funnel cake and offered it to me, I shook my head. "I need real food. Beck's got lobster rolls on the menu tonight. You want one?"

"Do lobsters have faces?"

"Um...yes?"

"Then that should answer the question."

"It really doesn't."

She shrugged, the move drawing my eyes to the bare expanse of her shoulder and that tattoo peeking out of her sweater. "I don't eat food with faces."

I blinked at her, certain I'd heard her wrong. "You don't...eat food...with faces."

"Nope. It just, I don't know, feels...weird."

"Chaining yourself to a tree doesn't feel weird, but consuming food with a face does?"

"Chaining myself to that tree felt awesome. Eating a formerly living being does not."

I hummed, swiping my thumb across the corner of her mouth to catch a drop of chocolate before sucking it clean. "And how long have you not eaten food with a face?"

"I don't know. As long as I can remember. Since I was eight, at least, if not longer."

"Your parents put up with that?"

She laughed, still noshing away on the funnel cake, licking her fingers like they were goddamn popsicles and making things quite difficult south of the belt for me. "What do you mean 'put up with that'? It's just vegetarian, and I was cooking for myself anyway."

I raised my brows. "You were cooking for yourself at eight?"

"You weren't?" she asked, without judgment but full of intrigue.

"No." While I certainly helped—as the oldest of six, I hadn't had a whole lot of choice in the matter—my parents still ran the household. At least, back then. Before.

193

"Yeah, I kind of had to figure it out. No siblings—older or otherwise. My mom's a little..." She squinted one eye as she chewed. "Flighty, I guess? She's me, but, like, a hundred times worse. And my dad's always worked long hours."

That was certainly different from the picture I'd painted of her upon first meeting. One of a spoiled little rich girl whose parents doted on her. Who got everything she wanted and never had to work for anything in her life. She'd grown up the exact opposite of me. While I hadn't had a moment's peace when I'd been younger, she'd had nothing but. And while I would've given anything for some solitude and privacy in my teen years, I wondered what it would've been like to basically be on my own that young.

"So you were alone a lot."

"Yeah."

"You don't sound sad about that."

She looked at me with curious eyes. "Why would I be?"

"You didn't mind it?"

"Not at all. As much as I love being around people, I adore being alone. I'm more myself when it's just me."

"You haven't been yourself when you're around me?" For some reason, that thought irritated me.

She paused for a minute, considering, then breathed out a laugh. "I actually have been, with you. I haven't been pulling my punches like usual. People get... I don't know. I usually have to water myself down to make myself more palatable to others. I'm too much, you know?"

"If anyone thinks you're too much, they can fuck off and find something less."

She blinked at me, a piece of funnel cake frozen in the air between the plate and her mouth. Then she shot her full-watt smile in my direction, and my heart cracked down the middle. Just split right in two.

"I think I need that on a bumper sticker." She grinned, knocking her shoulder into my chest. "Anyway, I haven't ever found anyone who accepts me as I am, completely. Besides my parents, anyway. They've always supported me and what I want to do."

"Like traveling around the country and protesting on a whim."

She laughed. "Exactly. Though that's not a surprise since both are in my blood. My mom's always been a free spirit, just going where the wind would take her, but if she was protesting, I was with her. She has a picture of the two of us from when I was maybe six months old, just strapped to her chest in a baby carrier while she marched."

"What about your dad?"

"He's not much for attending protests, but he supports us both. He's on the other side of the law, usually getting one of us out of trouble."

My brows flew up. "He's a cop?"

"Nope, lawyer. Pretty much as straitlaced as you are," she teased. "I have no idea how they work so well together. They just do. They've been together for thirty-five years.

Guess there's something to be said for that whole opposites attract thing."

My throat tightened, remembering what Beck had said about that very thing. Was that what was going on here? Why I felt so fucking drawn to her? Why I couldn't go a goddamn hour without thinking about her?

"That's...a different way to grow up," I finally said. "Being carted to protests, I mean."

"Is it?" She tipped her head to the side, studying me before finally shrugging. "It's all I've known, so it doesn't seem strange to me. I love that she encouraged that in me. Fighting for something you believe in is the most important thing you can do."

"Sorry to interrupt," someone called, and I turned to find Harper striding toward us.

"Harper, hey!" Luna twisted around and shot her a smile. "How're you feeling? You been drinking lots of water?"

Harper held up a half-full water bottle. "I'll be peeing like a racehorse before too long, but I'm doing as you ordered. And I feel *amazing*. Your hands are magic. I'll definitely be adding that to the article."

I narrowed my eyes at her. "Article?"

With a laugh, she held up a hand and shook her head. "I still haven't gotten an answer yet, but I can't help but take notes while I'm here. I've practically written the whole piece already, but that doesn't mean Starlight Cove will get the feature. I'm hoping it does, though."

"That's great to hear." Luna grinned.

"Not gonna lie," Harper said, "there wasn't a whole lot of love lost between me and this place, but I'm starting to see the appeal again."

"It grows on you, doesn't it? The town, I mean. I love it." Luna smiled, her gaze shifting to mine as she added quietly, "And all the people in it."

CHAPTER SEVENTEEN

LUNA

WAS THERE anything better than a small-town festival? No, there absolutely was not, and no one could convince me otherwise. Add in the fact that this festival was only yards from the beach, and I was completely smitten.

Brady and I had strolled down Main Street, and he'd surprised the hell out of me when he'd linked his fingers with mine as I'd dragged him into every tent while I sampled all the wares. And then he'd lugged all my purchases around before finally running back and dropping them at the car. We got a few curious glances—none more so than from Beck and Addison when we'd strode up, hand in hand, so he could get his lobster rolls and demand a vegetarian dish for me since I "couldn't live off funnel cakes alone" and I would just "be hangry later" if I didn't "eat some real goddamn food"—and I couldn't even blame them.

The sheriff and the woman he kept arresting? Impossible.

And yet, somehow...not.

I didn't know what had changed between us—maybe everything. Maybe nothing at all. Maybe our differences were exactly why this worked, just like with my parents. Exactly why whatever was happening between us didn't feel anything but right.

After a couple hours of mindless wandering, I could tell Brady was getting antsy. He wasn't exactly a people person, and being the county sheriff meant he knew everyone, and everyone knew him. We couldn't walk ten feet without someone calling out a greeting or stopping to say a quick—or not so quick—hello. And while I fed off the interaction, I could tell it drained him.

Finally, after the fifth interruption in the past ten minutes, I dragged him toward the beach. "Come on. We need a break."

"Where're we going?"

"Thought that was pretty obvious, Einstein." I swept my arm out in front of us, gesturing to the stretch of shore we were headed toward.

"This part of the beach closes at sunset."

I gasped, holding my hand in front of my mouth as I widened my eyes. "Oh no! What if we get arrested?"

"Luna..." he said in a low, warning tone.

I tugged him to a stop, tucked my hand into the front of his jeans, and pulled him closer. "Aw, come on, Sheriff.

You can play the big, bad cop later. I'll even let you cuff me."

"You're playing with fire, you know that?"

"I'm counting on it." I reached for his hand again, tugging him along behind me. This time, he came willingly.

It was darker out here, the lights from the festival barely reaching the shore and the waning crescent moon didn't provide much illumination, so I pulled out my phone, turned on the flashlight, and held it out to guide our way. Once we were far enough away that just the faintest hint of the music and the raucous laughter from festivalgoers reached us, I pocketed my phone, dropped to the sand, and pulled Brady down behind me. I fitted myself between his legs, leaning back against his chest and deeply inhaling the salty ocean air.

I shuddered, the breeze coasting in off the ocean chilling me, and Brady wrapped his arms around me, tugging me close and imbuing me with his warmth.

"If you planned to sit by the ocean at nine o'clock at night this time of the year, you should've dressed warmer," he grumbled against my neck.

"Why would I need to dress warmer when you're my own personal furnace? Besides, I didn't know we were going to come out here until I grabbed your hand and started walking this direction. I never plan anything."

"I've noticed."

"Yeah, yeah, you hate it and I drive you nuts. But where's the fun in planning everything?"

"I'm not looking to have fun. I'm looking to keep people safe."

"You're pretty good at that, you know." When all he gave was a grunt in response, I continued, "Like last night. Convincing me to go with you." I smiled when he just snorted. "Convincing me, dragging me away...tomato, tomahto. Either way, I'm glad I listened."

"Me too." The two words were so filled with emotion, they shot straight to the center of my chest.

I snuggled deeper into his embrace, tipping my head to the side to give him room to nuzzle my neck and remembering what Mrs. Engles had said earlier. About all the hardships Brady's family had faced and how something had changed him. "When you said people died in these storms, I thought you were being facetious. But you weren't, were you?"

He was quiet for several long moments, then he finally said, "No. I wasn't."

"Your mom?" I whispered.

"Yeah."

"Was she camping by the ocean, too?"

A heavy gust of air left him, and he tightened his arms around me. "Nope. I'd have found her if that was the case. I was on duty that night, so I wasn't at the resort. If I'd been there, I could've..." He exhaled a harsh breath. "I don't know. Nothing. Everything. I could've told her we had the goddamn rules in place for a reason. Forced her not to break them."

"What rules?"

"We only had two. Never sail alone, and never during a storm."

God, I could feel the anguish lacing his words. A picture suddenly materialized in my mind, an image of the gorgeous, auburn-haired beauty at the helm of a sail-boat in the middle of a ravaging sea, all alone. My heart ached. For him. For their whole family. For what they'd lost.

We were quiet for long moments, just the faint notes from the band and the sound of the waves filling up the space around us. And I let him just be. Offered him my strength in the silence.

After a few minutes, I said, "Tell me about her? What did she do?"

He was quiet for a long moment, and I worried I'd pushed too hard, reopened a wound that hadn't ever quite healed. But he surprised me when he answered, "She ran the resort. She loved it. It'd been in her family for three generations."

"Four now, with you and your siblings running it, right?"

"My siblings more than me, but yeah."

I didn't buy that—Brady may not have been at the resort for ten- or twelve-hour days, but I'd been around enough to see that not a day went by when he wasn't there, checking in on things. Not just with the resort, but with his siblings, as well.

"She was a sailor?"

"Yep. Taught us all. Levi took to it more than anyone, but we all know how."

"What about your dad?"

Brady stiffened, the subtle relaxation I'd managed to coax out of him gone in a blink. "He was a former factory worker, but he lost his job when the factory closed. And then everything went to hell."

I made a soft sound of commiseration. "I'm sure that was tough."

"Especially for an alcoholic. Especially after my mom died."

I knew if we weren't sitting like this, my back to his front, with the cloak of darkness shrouding us, he wouldn't be so open with me. With anyone. Just like I watered myself down so others could swallow me, Brady hid away the parts of himself he didn't want others seeing. He never let his guard down—hell, I wasn't sure he even allowed himself that vulnerability with his siblings—but he was now. With me. And I was nothing more than a starving woman, scrambling to pick up any morsel he dropped.

"Is that why you don't talk to him anymore?" Though I didn't have any real experience dealing with loved ones facing addiction—as long as you didn't count work or weed, which my dad and mom, respectively, were quite adept at—I'd had enough friends in school whose family members suffered from addiction, either alcohol, pills, or hard drugs. I'd seen firsthand the wreckage it could cause. Could understand why, in the wake of dealing with the fallout of something like that, especially following a parent's death, someone would grow fierce. Protective. Rigid and unbending. Controlled.

"I don't talk to him anymore because he wants it that way."

I linked our fingers together, brushing my thumb over the back of his hand, trying to give a tiny bit of peace back to him. "I'm sure that's not true."

"No?" He breathed out a humorless laugh. "Did you see a welcome mat in front of Cottage Thirteen? 'Cause I sure as hell didn't, even though I show up every week without fail."

My thumb froze against his hand, my entire body going still. Wait...the cottage he'd dropped groceries off at earlier today was his *dad's*?

"I didn't know he lived in Starlight Cove. I just assumed—"

"That a father wouldn't bail on his kids when times got tough? After they'd already lost one parent? Maybe most, but not mine."

I resumed the soft brush of my thumb against his skin, not knowing how much longer I had before he clammed up, but wanting to find out as much about him as I could. Wanted answers so I knew how to help. Knew what I could say or do that would make him feel better. "Does he speak to your siblings?"

"Nope. He's been nothing but a selfish bastard, but we still can't leave him behind."

"What do you mean?"

"We've all been doing little things for him, but I'm the only one who knows that particular secret."

"What kinds of little things? You bring him groceries?"

"And pay any bills he has. Beck drops off food from the diner. Addison changes out the porch flowers and decorations every season. Aiden brings him fresh linens and takes care of his laundry, and Ford leaves him a new book each week."

God, my heart ached for them. All of them. My parents had left me on my own for most of my life, encouraging my independence, but I never doubted they'd be there when and if I ever needed them to be. To know that your own father was right down the road but didn't care enough to even open the door when you stopped by had to be the worst kind of rejection. The worst kind of heartbreak. And it was one Brady faced each week, without fail.

"What about Levi?" I asked.

"He's the only one smart enough to leave Dad behind. I think he truly believes both our parents died when Mom did. Maybe one day, I'll get smart like him and stop."

I pulled out of his grasp and turned around, readjusting myself so I straddled his lap, his face held between my hands.

His short beard scratched against my palms, his lips soft under my thumb as I swept it across his mouth. It was too dark out here to see his eyes, but I knew if I could, they'd be filled with pain and sorrow. Knew, too, that was why he'd shared this with me in the first place, out here, where I couldn't see everything he tried so hard to hide from everyone else.

Everyone else but me.

"You won't," I said, pressing a soft kiss on his lips. "You won't stop."

"Don't be so sure." He slid his hands beneath the hem of my sweater, resting his palms against my bare back. "I've wanted to. Every fucking week, I tell myself that's the last time. And every fucking week, I go right back. Even when I want to, I can't break out of my goddamn routine."

"It's not about that." After all, wasn't this, right here and now, him breaking out of his routine? He sat on this beach, illegally, just because I'd asked him to. Wasn't *every-thing* where I was concerned him doing the very thing he claimed he could never do? He could, if he truly wanted to. Which meant only one thing. He didn't actually want to abandon his father, even though it was clear the man had already abandoned Brady.

"What's it about, then?" he asked, his voice gruff and filled with something I couldn't name.

"It's about you being a better man than he is. You not stopping has nothing to do with whatever routine you think you're stuck in and everything to do with the fact that you won't stop because you're too good. You're a good man, Brady. That's why you keep showing up. Even for someone who doesn't deserve it."

He was quiet for long moments, and I rested my hand on his chest, feeling the soft, soothing thud of his heartbeat beneath my palm. Finally, he cleared his throat, his voice raspy as he said, "Thought I was a pain in your ass."

I breathed out a laugh and wrapped my arms around him, squeezing him tight to me as I locked my ankles at his lower back. "The two aren't mutually exclusive. You can be both, as you've proven."

With my arms and legs wrapped around him, I rested my cheek on his shoulder, listening to the rhythm of the waves behind me. Brady held me snug to his chest, his hands under my sweater, arms tight bands of steel surrounding me, like he was afraid I'd disappear if he didn't hold me close enough.

He'd laid himself bare to me out here, and I knew that hadn't been easy for him. Knew, too, that he wouldn't want me to make a big deal out of it or fuss over him or what he'd told me. That wasn't who he was. So instead, I gave him the kind of distraction I knew he needed.

I shifted on top of him, canting my hips so I could slide against his length, and smiled as his fingers twitched on my back, his cock hardening beneath me.

He tucked his face close, his words a whispered breath against my ear. "Don't think I don't know what you're doing, lawbreaker."

"What?" I asked with as much innocence as I could

207

muster. Which, to be fair, wasn't much. "I'm just trying to get comfy."

He brushed his lips across my shoulder, and then he dug his teeth in sharp enough to make me gasp and grind down harder against him.

"Okay, that time I was trying to ride your dick."

With a groaned laugh, he suddenly stood with me in his arms, his hands palming my ass as he walked us back the way we came.

"What the hell?" I asked. "Where are we going?"

"Home."

"What if I wasn't ready yet?"

"Then you shouldn't have ground your pussy down on me like you wanted to get fucked on the beach."

"Was it that obvious? You sure I can't talk you into breaking another rule?"

"I'm not fucking you out here. Not unless you want me to rip a hole in your leggings, because I'm not taking them off. You'd be too cold."

God, this man. He was gruff and stoic, a rule-follower to the extreme and my complete opposite. But he was caring and considerate, would fight to the ends of the earth for the people he loved, even if he hid those parts of himself away, burying them under bravado and barked commands.

"A good man *and* a softy," I teased, wrapping my limbs tighter around him.

"You won't be saying that in about fifteen minutes."

I pulled back and grinned at him, catching my lower lip between my teeth as the lights from the festival softly illuminated his face. A face I'd come to love. His eyes were dark, heated. But I saw a warmth in their depths that hadn't been there before. Warmth for me.

I refused to think about what that meant. Or what it'd do to him when I left.

CHAPTER EIGHTEEN

LUNA

BACK AT BRADY'S HOUSE, I stepped out of the hall bathroom and headed toward the guest room, stopping dead in my tracks before I made it through the doorway. The bed had been stripped and was now just a bare mattress, and my bag wasn't anywhere to be found.

Cocking my head to the side, I made my way to Brady's room, and sure enough, my bag sat on the floor on my side of the bed. Though, truth be told, when I'd slept in here last night, Brady's side *was* my side. I hadn't left the warmth of his body the entire time.

"Did you kick me out of my accommodations, Sheriff?"

Brady looked up from where he set his phone on his nightstand, his gaze sweeping me from head to toe. Then he strode toward me, a white piece of fabric clutched in his hand. "If you think you're sleeping anywhere but my bed

210

after I saw your van smashed within an inch of its life this morning, you haven't been paying attention."

As soon as he stood in front of me, he gripped the hem of my sweater and pulled it up and over my head, his eyes heating when he found me bare beneath it. "You always go out in public like this?" he asked as he circled his thumb around my nipple.

With a grin, I arched toward him, my body yearning for more. "I'm not sure if you've noticed this, Sheriff, but I don't exactly have a need for support."

He leaned down, engulfing a nipple in his mouth and sucking deep, pulling a gasp straight from my lips. "What I've noticed is your tits are perfect."

Instead of continuing with his torture, he pulled the T-shirt over my head and covered me. Then he dropped to his knees—this big, beautiful, scowly man—and slid my leggings down over my hips until they pooled at my ankles, his brow lifting when he found I was wearing panties.

I rolled my eyes, bracing a hand on his shoulder as I lifted first one leg, then the other, letting him undress me. "I wasn't going to be bare-assed while I was leading a one-on-one yoga class for Harper."

He lifted the hem of the T-shirt he'd dressed me in, then pressed a kiss to my bare hip. "That's fine, but you're not wearing them in my bed."

Then he stood, hauling me over his shoulder and chuckling lowly at my yelp. In three long strides, I was airborne before bouncing on the mattress as giggles erupted from me. My laughter died on my lips as soon as our gazes met. He reached behind his head and pulled off his shirt in one smooth motion. His jeans went next, and then he shut off the light before he crawled in beside me wearing nothing but black boxer briefs that did little to hide his reaction to me.

But instead of pouncing on me like I thought he would, he gathered me in close, my back resting against his chest, and tucked his legs beneath mine so every inch of me was touching some part of him.

I exhaled on a sigh, not realizing I'd needed this until he'd given it to me. The past twenty-four hours had been a roller-coaster ride, from Brady showing up in the storm to him dragging me away to having the best sex of my life—*twice*—with the man I wasn't supposed to get along with, let alone actually care about, to finding my home crushed beneath a tree. Not to mention the secrets he'd shared, opening up to me in a way I knew he didn't with others. But he had with me. For some reason, he'd seen me as someone worthy of those secrets.

He saw me, too, as someone worthy of his concern.

He'd shown me that in a dozen different ways, but it'd taken a tree falling on my van for me to finally see it. I wasn't used to being cared for like this. Wasn't used to being...treasured.

My stomach felt like a rocket launched into space, a volcano ready to erupt. I didn't know how Brady and I fit together, only that we did. Had no idea how this could ever work between us, only that I wanted it to.

As we lay there, I felt the tension leave his body, his lips pressed against the back of my neck, nose buried in my hair, as if reminding himself I was here. I was safe.

"Did you tell your parents?" he asked after a while.

"That I'm lying in bed with you? No. But I could call them now if you want."

He shifted and tweaked my nipple, pulling a gasped laugh from me. "About your van, smartass."

"Hmm? Oh, no. I talked to my mom this morning before I knew about it."

"Are you going to tell them?"

"Why would I?"

He grunted, and there must've been some crazy voodoo magic working between us, because I could tell just from that single non-syllable that he wasn't happy about that.

I ran my fingers over his forearm that was locked across my chest, holding me to him. "I've been looking after myself for a long time, Brady."

He grumbled something under his breath, and when I asked him to speak up, he said, "You shouldn't always have to look after yourself. Someone else should be looking out for you too."

"And who should that someone else be?"

He tightened his arms around me and brushed his lips

across the length of my neck, his unspoken *me* as loud as if he'd screamed it.

"I might be on board with something like that. What does this looking out for me entail? Are we talking about, like, morning smoothies? Or just orgasms?"

He slid his hand under my shirt and cupped one of my breasts, brushing his thumb over the already hardened peak. "Why not both?"

"I don't want to be greedy."

He breathed out a laugh and snaked his hand down my stomach to cup my bare pussy, his finger sliding between my lips and teasing my clit. "We both know that's a lie. Your pussy's greedy as hell, isn't it?"

"Only for you, apparently." I gasped and rocked into his hand, stroking myself faster over his questing finger. "I guess it likes when *someone* looks out for me."

He groaned into my neck even as he dipped a finger inside me before dragging the wetness up and circling my clit again. "This wasn't supposed to happen."

"No?" I asked, breathless and arching into him already. "That why you took my panties?"

"I just wanted to hold you tonight," he said against my skin, his voice so low, I barely heard him. But I did. I heard every word—what he was saying aloud as well as everything unspoken between us. Brady needed a reminder that I was okay. That whatever irrational fears he'd harbored following his mother's death hadn't been relived with me.

While he hadn't been able to save either of his parents from their demises, he'd saved me.

"Why can't we do both?" I reached back and slipped my hand into his boxers, finding him ready for me. His cock was long and thick and so deliciously hard, I needed him inside me. I pulled him out of his boxer briefs as I arched against him, lifting my leg and hooking it back over his, opening myself up to him and whatever he wanted to do to me.

He slid into me then, filling me in slow, deep thrusts. It was unhurried and languid, a soft, sleepy fuck that I didn't know I'd needed after the day I'd had but melted into anyway. But somehow, he'd known. He read me so well, studied every cue I'd ever given, and stored all that information away, just so he'd know what I needed. Just so he could pull it out at any time and give it to me.

My orgasm grew slowly, a steady climb that built with each gentle thrust of him inside me, with each circle of his fingers against my clit, with each soft brush of his lips against my neck, my ear, my jaw.

"Brady..." I breathed, reaching up to slide my fingers into his hair, needing his mouth on mine. Needing to be as connected to him as I possibly could when he made me fall apart.

"I've got you, pretty girl," he said before he pressed his lips to mine, his tongue sweeping into my mouth as the world exploded around me.

And he did have me. In everything, not just this. Not

just my body, but my heart, too. My soul. I didn't know how it'd happened, but somewhere along the way, between our bickering and banter, our fighting and fucking, I'd fallen for the grumpy sheriff of a town where I'd never intended to stay.

CHAPTER NINETEEN

BRADY

FOR THE PAST FOUR DAYS, I'd woken up with Luna in my arms, and each morning had only gotten better. It was hard to believe after the way we'd started that this was the routine we'd fallen into. But we had. Somehow, against all odds, this was where we'd found ourselves.

And it was as easy as breathing.

I'd leave Luna in the mornings, sometimes with a kiss and sometimes without the ability to make her rouse at all, and then come home after my shift to an absolute disaster. While Luna had been spending more time at the resort, leading at least one yoga class every day, thanks to the interest piqued from Mabel's Live during goat yoga, as well as massages as requested, she'd also taken advantage of the new workspace—read: my house—available to her. Word had spread about homemade ointments, and now Mabel and her entire gang of misfits had commissioned a buttload of creams from Luna, and she was all too willing to comply.

That was all fine and good, except that it meant my kitchen was no longer the tidy and uncluttered space it'd always been. But it wasn't just my kitchen. Not an inch of my home had been untouched by what Addison had deemed the Luna sparkle. There was incense and jars filled with something called moon water that just looked like plain old water to me and rocks every-fucking-where, and I...didn't hate it.

Had, in fact, brought her all the shit in the first place, so I only had myself to blame.

But seeing her come to my home with one sad little bag when her whole life was in that van had cracked something inside me. So, before Frank could tow it away, I'd scavenged what I could from it. Rocks, essential oils, scarves, and too many bracelets to count, just to name a few. She hadn't been in any sort of state of mind to remember those things when we'd come to find her home crushed, but I knew they were important to her.

That meant they were important to me.

Harper had left the morning after we'd run into her at the festival, and Addison had received an email late yesterday afternoon saying they'd have a decision by the end of the day today. Which meant we'd made it. What had started as merely a distraction for the world's most chaotic woman had ended in something more real than I'd ever thought was possible.

"If you were going to think so hard so early in the morning, I wish you'd get out of bed to do it," Luna mumbled from where she lay curled against me, her face smashed into my chest. She didn't even crack an eye, didn't move a single muscle either. The woman definitely loved her sleep. Loved sleeping in, too, which was why her varied and loosely regulated schedule at the resort worked perfectly for her.

I reached down and palmed her bare ass, pressing my lips to her forehead. "That's not the only thing that's hard around here."

She pressed her face into my chest, smothering her laughter, though her body shook against mine. My lips curved at the sound, loving this gentle, sleepy side to her. Hell, I was finding there wasn't a side to her I didn't.

And that scared the shit out of me.

I didn't give my love freely...or at all. Hadn't in years. Love had only led to loss in my eyes. It meant heartbreak and pain and abandonment. But no matter what I'd done, no matter the blockades I'd put in place to keep people out, I still hadn't been able to stop the inevitable. From the first moment I'd set eyes on Luna, she'd sparked something in me. Something fierce and wild and something I'd shoved down for too long. It had been a losing game from day one.

"Well, are you gonna do something about that, Sheriff, or do you have more important places to be?" she asked, walking her fingers down my stomach until she gripped my cock, stroking up the length and passing her thumb over the head, making me groan into her hair.

Before I could roll over, pin her beneath me, and sink inside, my phone rang with Aiden's ringtone, and I stilled.

"You need to get that?" she asked, moving her hand faster over my length.

Forcing down the urge to look, I focused instead on the gorgeous woman whose hand was wrapped around my cock. "Nope."

"Ohh, being naughty." She grinned. "I like it."

While she stroked me, driving me out of my mind with need, I rained kisses down her neck and to her bare tits, sucking one nipple into my mouth as the phone stopped ringing. Thank God. I'd just switched to the other when it started up all over again.

I swore into her skin, her laughter shaking her body beneath me. Lifting my head, I stared down into her smiling face. Her hair was loose, the dark mass a riot against my pillow, her eyes still sleepy and soft, and I wanted to bury myself inside her and never leave. Wanted to kiss every inch of her body, make her come against my tongue, and then fuck her slow and sweet. To hell with the rest of the world. To hell with my responsibilities. I was off today anyway. I could miss one family meeting, and the world wouldn't come to an end.

So I ignored everything else but her. I silenced my phone, dove under the covers, and affixed my mouth to her pussy. In minutes, Luna was crying out my name, her fingers gripping my hair as she rode out her orgasm against my tongue.

When I slipped inside her moments later, her pussy still fluttering with her release, I stared down at her and wondered how the hell we'd managed to end up here. This woman, who'd spent the first month we'd known each other driving me out of my mind with frustration, had somehow slipped past my barriers. Had somehow settled herself into my life like she'd always been there, making me wonder how I'd survived without her.

Soft and slow, I rocked us both to our climaxes, our mouths open, lips connected as we came together. After, while we both caught our breath, she lay on my chest, her cheek puffing up against me as she smiled.

"What?" I asked, trailing my fingers up and down the expanse of her bare back.

Resting her arm on my chest, she propped her chin on the back of her hand and stared at me, eyes glittering. "Nothing. You're just breaking out of your routine left and right. Last night, it was popcorn in bed, and now, you missed the morning meeting? Pretty soon, I'll have you smoking pot on your back deck. I'm a bad influence on you."

"You're something, all right," I said, reaching down to swat her ass.

With a laugh, she rolled away, leaped down from the bed, and strolled to the en suite bathroom, completely uncaring that she was naked and had an enraptured audience. I stared after her until she shut the door, then blindly reached for my phone to see what I'd missed.

Four calls and two texts, from Aiden and Addison, which wasn't a surprise, given my lack of appearance at the meeting for the first time in...ever. Addison's text just said *Do something!* So I scrolled to Aiden's for more context.

Turn on Mabel's Live. Now.

I navigated to the app on my phone and browsed until I found the Live. My brows furrowed when the video popped up. It was just shaky footage of the ground, like someone had forgotten they were recording as they walked, and I couldn't make out the murmur of voices. Then the scene came into focus, the camera suddenly upright, and Mabel's disembodied voice filtered through the phone.

"What brings you to our neck of the woods?"

"Our daughter," a woman said, her head cut off thanks to Mabel's less than stellar recording skills, though I didn't recognize her voice.

"Your daughter's made quite the ruckus in our little town. Are you here to chain yourself to a tree, too?"

The door to the bathroom opened and Luna stepped out, but I couldn't tear my gaze away from the screen, the knot in my stomach tightening with every second that passed.

"If that's what it takes," the unknown woman said. "Her father and I are happy to support her, every step of the way."

At the sound of the woman's voice, Luna rushed to the bed, her eyes wide. She grabbed the phone from me, her mouth dropping open. "Mom?"

"Mom?" I repeated, tone incredulous as I stared at the woman I'd bared my soul to. Told my deepest, darkest secrets to. The one who'd promised me her help.

The one who'd, apparently, sold us out and decided her whims were more important than the future of my family's legacy.

What. The fuck.

With her eyes glued on the screen, Luna mumbled something, but I couldn't pay attention. Couldn't hear what she was saying through the loud *whoosh whoosh whoosh* in my ears. This couldn't be happening. The *one* time I didn't follow my plan, didn't show up where I was expected to, and it ended like this. If I'd been there at the meeting, I could've gotten to the site early, cut them off before anything had been broadcast. Instead, I'd been love drunk, uncaring of anything besides sliding inside Luna.

What the hell was wrong with me?

I shot out of bed, tugging on clothes as I went, ignoring the lancing pain in my chest. This was un-fucking-believable. We'd needed *one* more day. One more day of peace so this article on the resort would get pushed through, and she couldn't even give us that.

I stormed toward the door, intent on getting down to the Williamsons' property as fast as humanly possible.

With my sirens if I had to. All I knew was I needed to fix this, and I needed to do it quickly.

"Wait, I'll go with you," Luna said, tucking my phone into my pocket before fluttering around the room, trying to find her clothes. "Just let me get dressed."

I stopped on the threshold of the door, not bothering to turn around, unable to look at her. "We were so close. How could you?"

"How could I what?" Luna asked, the sound of clothes rustling behind me nearly enough to make me turn, but I was frozen. Anger and hurt and betrayal coursing through me, making my feet blocks of cement.

I breathed out a disbelieving laugh and shook my head. "Right. Like you had nothing to do with this. Your parents just *happened* to show up in Starlight Cove, at the site you've been protesting, to fight the same thing you've been fighting. The same thing you *promised* me you'd lay off. Just until the article came through. You knew how important this was to my family. To *me*."

She rested a hand on my back, and I nearly flinched at the touch, hating myself that, even now, I wanted to lean into it. To seek comfort from it. "I know it is. And Brady, I didn't—"

"Save it," I said, my voice too harsh, but I couldn't rein in my temper. Pissed at her for what she'd done, and pissed at myself that I'd lost sight of what was most impor- tant. That I'd loosened the restraints on my control and let her slip past my defenses. That I'd let her steer me away from what needed to be done. From what was most important. "After everything I told you on the beach, you still went and did this."

"No, Brady. I—"

But I didn't hear the rest of what she said. I couldn't. I couldn't stand there another second and listen to whatever lie she wanted to tell. Whatever narrative would fit what she wanted. Not when my family's livelihood was on the line. Not when I was about to watch my mother's legacy go down in flames.

Instead, I typed out a text to Aiden, letting him know I was on the way, and stormed down the stairs and out the door, not looking back as I climbed into my car. Before I pulled out, a text from Aiden popped up on my screen. Just two little words, but they lit a fire inside me.

Fix it.

That was my job—as both the sheriff and the head of my family—and it was exactly what I intended to do. I just had to figure out how.

I'D JUST PULLED up to the Williamsons' property when my phone rang. Again. Luna had been trying in vain to contact me, and I'd let them all go to voice mail. Now, I glanced down, seeing the mayor's name on the screen, and closed my eyes on a groan. At least I didn't have to reject another call from Luna, but this wasn't much better. I didn't have time for this, but I couldn't exactly ignore it.

There were already cars all over the place, way more than I'd assumed would be here, which could only mean one thing—news had spread like wildfire, and I was about to get my ass reamed.

"Mayor Drummond," I answered.

"Sheriff McKenzie," she said, her tone clipped. "I understand you're not on duty today, but justice doesn't wait for a schedule."

"Justice doesn't get doled out when it's convenient, either. I just got here, but right now, it's just a bunch of residents congregating."

She huffed. "Yeah, well, it's all fun and games until the reporters show up."

I stepped out of my car and scanned the crowd, swearing under my breath when I spotted Harper at the door of Holton Group's trailer, her hand raised to knock. "Guess it's not fun and games anymore, then."

The mayor expelled a heavy sigh, her disappointment ringing loud and clear through the line. "This doesn't look good for the town, Sheriff. Whatever is going on down there, you need to put a stop to."

"If they're protesting peacefully, I can't do anything. Not unless Holton Group comes and presses charges, and they've been absent for the past two weeks."

"Not for long. I just received a call, and the foreman is on the way."

"Fantastic. Can't wait." The guy was an asshole, and I hated dealing with him, but I might not have a choice.

"Look, Sheriff, when we had the town hall meeting, everyone was excited about the shopping center."

I glanced around at the growing number of Starlight Cove residents, some with handmade signs that said some variance of *Stop the Development*. "I'm not sure everyone feels that way now."

"Unfortunately, that's not how things work. What's done is done. The deal's already been made. The land's been sold, and we've approved the plans. Holton Group is only unable to move forward right now because of the paperwork *you* rushed through."

"Paperwork I rushed through on behalf of a concerned citizen. I'm doing my job."

"Do it better."

I gritted my teeth against the words that wanted to spill out, this constant pressure in my chest making it hard to think. I *was* doing my goddamn job, but what was I supposed to do when they all conflicted with one another? Right now, I couldn't be the sheriff of Starlight Cove, the patriarch of the McKenzie family, and Luna's...whatever the hell I was to her, without disappointing one or more.

Her tone softened as she said, "I appreciate what you've done for this town, Sheriff, but we've got a long way to go. Everyone will be on board when they realize how convenient the new store will be. No need to run to five different places. Just remind everyone of that, of why they wanted it in the first place. And then shut down whatever nonsense is happening over there."

I ground my teeth together, frustration making my words too harsh as I said, "I can't just shut it down. That's not how things work. There's nothing illegal going on. Right now, the only person on the Williamsons' property is Harper, and she's with the press. All the residents are clumped on the resort side, so it doesn't matter if Holton Group is on their way or not. They can't charge anyone with trespassing."

"They can't, but *you* can. That's your family's property. Your *mom's legacy*," she said, enunciating the words like they hadn't been a constant litany in my head already. "I thought you loved this town as much as she did."

Her words had the effect she'd no doubt intended, slicing straight through to my heart. My mom had given Levi his love for sailing, Aiden his love for the resort, Ford his love for building, Beck his love for cooking, and Addison her love for flowers. But she'd given me my love for this town.

I glanced up, spying a car as it rolled to a slow stop near the road, and out ran Luna, tossing money through the opened driver's side window. My heart seized at the sight. Her hair was in disarray, pillow creases still marring her cheek, as she frantically scanned the crowd. For what or whom, I didn't know.

God, I was furious with her. Furious she'd done what she'd done and hadn't talked to me about it. Warned me, at least. Furious she'd put the resort's future in jeopardy. And furious with myself that I'd fallen for her in the first place.

I cleared my throat. "I do love this town. And the residents." One spitfire of a woman in particular, but I didn't need to share that with the mayor.

"Then fix this." With that, she hung up, and I was left staring at the pain in my ass I'd somehow fallen head over heels in love with and wondering what the fuck was the right thing to do.

CHAPTER TWENTY

MY STOMACH WAS in knots as I rode in the back seat of some rando's car. Okay, so he wasn't a total rando. His name was Arthur, and he seemed very nice. The vehicle was clean enough, with a ripped notebook page taped to the inside corner of the windshield that said simply NON-UBER in shaky blue marker. He was a tiny man who looked old enough to have been around when dinosaurs roamed the earth, and he couldn't have been driving more than twenty miles an hour. But considering he was the one and only non-Uber driver in town, I didn't have much of a choice. Not when my van was in the shop and Brady had stormed out of his house without a word or a backward glance.

"I hear there's a big to-do out there on the Williamsons' property," Arthur said as we crawled through town, stopping for a solid ten seconds at each of the two empty intersections we'd come across. "Something about puppies being chained to the trees without food or water for days on end?"

I rolled my eyes, knowing that was just Mabel's embellishment of the situation—what situation, I didn't know, but I was about ninety-five percent sure it didn't involve puppies. "Don't believe everything you hear on Facebook, Arthur," I muttered, dialing Brady again, though I knew it'd be in vain.

I'd tried calling him twelve times, and he'd ignored all twelve calls. I needed to tell him I didn't know what the hell my parents were doing in Starlight Cove, why they'd shown up at the Williamsons' property, or why Mabel was with them, just that I didn't have anything to do with it. I'd kept my end of the deal...a deal I wasn't so sure I should've made in the first place.

I wasn't fighting for something frivolous here. I was fighting for what I believed in, and I'd set that aside for him. There was no denying that we had a fundamental difference of opinion on most things. Brady wanted me quiet and compliant...even if just for a while. But wasn't that exactly what everyone wanted from me?

Just be a little less loud, a little less opinionated, a little less blunt, a little less bubbly or vivacious or dramatic. Just. Be. Less.

I'd thought it had been different with Brady, but hadn't he been trying to do the same thing the entire time we'd known each other? Hadn't he been trying to force me into a perfect little box and behave?

That wasn't who I was, and it wasn't who I wanted to be. Not even for him. Not even for the man who'd stolen my heart and held it hostage in his stoic hands.

I still believed in everything I'd been protesting—to prevent Holton Group from razing twenty acres of wildlife just for a shopping center the town didn't need in the first place—but I didn't want it to come at the expense of Brady and his family.

That didn't change that this wasn't the right choice for Starlight Cove and all the people in it—Brady's family included. But all he saw was black-and-white. Good or bad. Wrong or right. He couldn't see into the shades of gray where most things lived, this included. While, yes, the development may have been good in the short-term, people would suffer in the long-term. In ten years, this town wouldn't hold any of its original charm. The family-owned businesses would be gone, eradicated by one large conglomerate.

And I knew him well enough to know he wouldn't want that.

"Here we are," Arthur said, pulling up alongside a cluster of cars.

I barely waited until he'd come to a complete stop before I jumped out. Not being actually affiliated with any of the rideshare apps meant he took only cash, so I tossed some bills his way before I dashed to the small but growing crowd of people. I needed to find Brady. Needed to tell him he'd jumped to the wrong conclusion while also convincing him this wasn't the awful endeavor he thought it was. Convincing him to listen to his heart instead of his head.

Standing on tiptoe, I searched around the area, looking for the tall grump with a glower that could make grown men wet themselves, but before I could spot him, an all too familiar voice squealed from behind me. "My baby!"

I didn't even have time to turn around before her arms surrounded me from behind, the familiar scent of sage and lavender washing over me.

"I've missed you!" she said, walking around to my front and holding me at arm's length, a bright smile on her face. "Are you surprised?"

"That's one way of putting it," I said, peeking around her as I searched for Brady. Normally, I would've been thrilled to see my parents—Mom, especially—but I had more pressing issues right now. Namely, finding my grump and making him see reason. "I wish you would've warned me."

Mom's brow furrowed as she regarded me. "I did warn you. I said your dad and I should take a trip up this way."

I rolled my eyes, spotting my dad talking to Mabel several yards away, her camera trained on his chest, probably cutting off his face as she was wont to do. To Mom, I said, "Yes, but you've also told me you were moving to Dubai, getting a phoenix rising tattoo over your entire back, and going to learn how to speak Mandarin, yet not a single one has happened."

She laughed, swatting a hand on my arm. "Well, you know me..." She shrugged. "Fickle as can be. Aren't you happy to see us?"

"I am. I just..." I waved my hand around, encompassing the crowd. "This is a lot of attention. Did you hear what I said about this? I told you I was laying low, waiting for the discovery to pan out."

"Yes, honey, I heard you." Mom scoffed. "I *do* listen when you talk, you know."

I wasn't so sure about that. Mom tended to hear exactly what she wanted to. "If that's true, then why'd you come *here*?"

She lifted a single shoulder. "Your dad wanted to take a peek, and we didn't think it would be a big to-do. We stopped by that cute little café in town when we arrived, and this nice lady was all too happy to show us where to go."

Mabel. Goddamn meddling old woman.

"Besides, getting coverage like this will only help your cause, right?"

"I'm trying to keep this *out* of the news for right now. But Mabel's Facebook videos aren't exactly going to make headlines."

"Oh, but she's not the only one here. There's another woman. The one who showed us how to get here. Tall, blond, gorgeous in that aloof sort of way," Mom said distractedly as she glanced around. "Now, where did she go..."

Harper. It had to be. I didn't know why she was back already, or why she'd helped my parents find this place, but those were the least of my worries. Not when she had the ability to sway the article one way or another. Not when I could paint this town in a different light—not as one of troublemakers, but of a family of concerned citizens, only wanting what was best for the town.

Brady may have wanted me to shut my mouth and behave like a good girl, to make me fit neatly into his life, but that wasn't me. And I wasn't going to sit idly by when I could make a difference. I just hoped he would come to understand that.

"I need to talk to her." I pushed away from my mom and traversed the ever-growing crowd, always on the lookout for Harper's head of blond hair.

I finally found her, talking to my dad, of all people. He was studying some papers, his reading glasses on the end of his nose, as Harper stood by, tapping her phone against her thigh.

"Harper," I said, my voice too tight to be considered friendly, but I couldn't help it.

"Luna, hey." She smiled at me. "I'm glad you're here."

"Hi, sweetheart," my dad said, not bothering to look up from the papers he was focused on. "Just give me a minute while I read through..." He trailed off, such as was the usual with him when it came to work, and I focused my attention back on Harper.

"I was just coming to find you," she said. "I wanted to—"

"Wait. Please." I held up my hand to stop her, ignoring the growing crowd behind us. I couldn't think about who was back there...if Brady was back there. "I need to say this first. Your magazine is looking for a compelling story, right?" Without waiting for her response, I continued, arm outstretched and gesturing to those gathered behind us. "Well, what's more compelling than a community coming together? Because that's what's here. That's what's happening. We might not always agree, but I'm certain every single person in Starlight Cove only wants the best for this town, whatever they think that may be.

"I love it here. I love this town, and I love the residents." Then, under my breath, I said, "One in particular, even if he is a stubborn ass most of the time and too much of a rule-follower to step out of line and question whether the status quo is right or wrong."

"Okay..." Harper said, drawing out the word. "There's a whole lot to unpack there."

"I'm not done." I pointed to the trailer that housed Holton Group's on-site office. "I know what they will do to this town. What this development will do. I've seen it too many times in countless small towns I've visited. That shopping center will put the Handy Mart out of business. Not to mention the hardware store, the grocery store, the bakery, and half a dozen others. And I don't have to have lived here for a decade to know that's not what the residents want. Starlight Cove isn't about chain establishments. It's about family legacies, and allowing this chain store to be built will only ruin that."

"You make some excellent points, but I need to—"

"Still more," I said, holding up my hand. I took a deep breath, knowing I was about to either make the worst mistake of my life or have a happy accident because God knew I hadn't planned a single word of this. "You should do the feature on the resort because it has beautiful cottages steps from the ocean, the best farm-to-table omelets I've ever had, a personal yoga instructor, and in-room massages given by the best massage therapist in Maine."

"You *are* very good," Harper said.

I sniffed. "Thank you. Now, if my protesting this development looks bad for an article about a place that's supposed to be the ideal small-town getaway, then your article is dumb as hell, and so is the magazine you're writing for. Starlight Cove deserves the feature. The resort deserves the feature. My doing this *proves* it's the perfect town—one worth fighting for. And I'm going to fight for it. Even if that means I have to chain myself to that tree every day for the foreseeable future and continue to get arrested by the grumpy-ass sheriff."

Harper stared at me for long moments after I'd

finished speaking, eyebrows raised. "Are you...are you done? Can I speak now?"

I exhaled a deep sigh, shoulders sagging. I'd said my piece. I'd taken a stand. Now, I could only hope for the best. "Go for it."

"Great." She grinned. "Excellent speech. Very moving. But there's something you're going to want to see."

CHAPTER TWENTY-ONE

BRADY

I STOOD off to the side while Luna delivered her impassioned speech, my heart splitting right in two, cracking further with each word out of her mouth. While she'd probably intended to speak to just Harper, she'd gathered quite a crowd as she'd spoken, my family and me included. Aiden, Beck, Ford, and Addison had shown up right as Luna had gotten on a roll. Levi was even here, propped on a tree a few feet away. And now they stood silently behind me, and I had no idea where their heads were.

Hell, I didn't know where *my* head was.

I'd lived my life as one of order and control, shouldering responsibility like it was my mission. I'd taken on the responsibility of this town, of the resort, of my family, without thought or concern for anything else.

And then Luna had swept in and opened my eyes to

something else entirely. She'd made me see. She'd made me *see*.

It didn't have to be all-or-nothing, black-or-white. She was every color of the rainbow and unapologetic about it. It was what had drawn me to her in the first place—what I thought I'd hated had come to be what I loved most about her.

And fuck. Yeah. I loved her. More than I thought possible, more than I could've ever hoped. There was no denying that anymore. She was settled so deep into my heart, I didn't think I'd ever be able to push her out. Didn't think I'd ever want to. I loved her sparkle and shine, her sass and her smart mouth. I loved how she goaded me, how she pushed me and challenged me. I loved how she listened, how she cared so deeply—for everything and everyone.

And yet, I'd doubted her. Accused her of something I'd known in my heart she'd never do.

But worse than all of that, I'd asked her to become something she wasn't. I'd done the very thing she'd told me people had been trying to do to her her whole life—I'd wanted her watered-down.

While she may have gone through life on the whims of a breeze, her principles were deeply rooted and unshakable. She didn't care how difficult it made things, and she refused to make herself smaller for anyone. The other night, she'd told me no one had stuck around, no one had taken her as is because she was *too much*. And I'd asked the same goddamn thing of her. Demanded it of her.

"Jesus, what the fuck did I do?" I mumbled, rubbing a hand over my tight chest.

Not just what did I do, but how did I fix it?

I needed to fix it because every word she'd said had rung true. Even I could admit that. If a national chain set up shop in Starlight Cove, all the mom-and-pop stores would feel the hit—there was no denying that. Just like my family had when those investors had come and flipped the properties along the beach, taking our meager income with them.

Fuck, I'd been an idiot not to just hear her out in the first place. I'd been too in my head, too focused on what I thought was right instead of what *felt* right.

"Sheriff, what are your thoughts on this?" Mabel asked, pulling my gaze away from Luna. She held a phone in front of my face, her brows raised. "You're not in uniform, but do you have your cuffs on you to start doling out arrests? You'll need an awful lot, considering the size of this crowd."

"I'm not going to arrest anyone," I said, searching the crowd for Luna, just so I had eyes on her. "I wish you'd stop stirring up shit just because you can."

"You're no fun." She pursed her lips. "You want to get people to the resort, right? Maybe an interview is how to do it. Did you ever think of that? Or maybe Starlight Cove's perpetual bachelor should take off his shirt and give the viewers a show."

"Mabel, I'm not—"

She sniffed. "I was talking about Ford."

At my brother's chuckle, I dug the heels of my palms into my eyes, a frustrated groan leaving me. "Mabel, I've turned a blind eye to George's and your late-night beach activities, but I won't be as accommodating in the future if you don't leave me alone."

Mabel's eyes went wide, and she breathed out a nervous laugh. "Point taken, Sheriff. I'll just see if—"

And then she was gone and off to harass some other poor, unsuspecting residents.

I turned my back on the crowd and spun to face my siblings. All of them were watching me, looking for answers. Even Levi, whose sunglasses shielded his eyes, was looking to me to lead along with the rest of them—because that was how it'd been since Mom had died. Since Dad had checked out. And I'd done it without question or hesitancy. For ten years, I'd been doing what I thought was right. But sometimes right wasn't black-or-white, and sometimes leading meant making the hard decisions. Sometimes you had to follow your heart instead of your head.

"This isn't what she would've wanted," I said quietly, Luna's words ringing in my ears and firming my resolve. "Mom, I mean. She would've hated this. Yes, the resort is her family's legacy—*our* family's legacy—and she loved it with everything she had. But she wouldn't have wanted the resort to succeed if it was at the expense of the town. Can you honestly say that's what you'd want?"

I clenched my jaw as I stared at them, none of them giving anything away. "That's exactly what will happen if we keep sitting by and doing nothing about this development. Worse, if we *encourage* it like we have been.

"You can't tell me this feels right. It hasn't. Not since day one when Holton Group first showed up and started touting all the benefits of this mega-center. I just thought that niggle in the back of my head was because of what those house flippers did to us, but it was more than that. It's not a good fit for the town. You heard what Luna said. What we'd be looking at in a few years' time. A totally different Starlight Cove. Is all of that worth it just so the resort succeeds?"

I glanced back at the growing crowd, at the beautiful, lush property we stood on, and shook my head. "Not to mention, did you know this particular piece of land has, like, forty different species of mammals and birds, too many plants to count, and removes over fifty tons of carbon dioxide each year?"

Beck's brows flew up. "Did you memorize all that for this speech?"

"Luna told me." Jesus, just the sound of her name on my lips had my chest aching. I needed to find her. Needed to get to her and tell her I fucked up. Beg her for forgiveness and promise I'd never ask her to be something she wasn't again, if only she'd give me another chance.

I ran a hand through my hair and glanced to each of my siblings in turn. "I know this goes against the plan, and it isn't what we were hoping for, but we can find another way. One that doesn't force us to choose between the town and the resort." I reached up and rubbed a hand over my heart, trying to ease the ache to no avail. "One that doesn't force me to choose between my family and the woman I never saw coming. One that doesn't feel like I've ripped a goddamn hole in my chest. I know you don't agree with Luna, but she's right." I dropped my arm and held my hands out, palms up. "Even if she weren't, I'd choose her. I have to choose her. She's it for me."

My siblings were quiet for long moments, their expressions giving nothing away except that all five of them were staring at me like I'd grown a third head.

Finally breaking the silence, Levi said, "Holy shit, I've never heard him say that much at once in my whole life."

"It's Luna," Beck answered with a nod. "She makes him chatty."

"She makes him something, all right." Ford clapped a hand on my shoulder and winked. "Getting laid regularly suits you."

"All right, that's enough of that." Addison crossed her arms and fixed each of us with a glare. "I could go my whole life without knowing any detail at all about my brothers' sex lives and be perfectly content. Thrilled, even. So, let's work on that, huh?"

Ford opened his mouth, probably to torment our baby sister, but Aiden slapped a hand on his chest, holding him back.

He met my eyes, his head cocked to the side as he studied me. "You love her."

Even though he didn't ask it like a question, I still answered anyway. "More than anything."

I held my breath as they regarded me, knowing I'd done the right thing and hoping they'd see it that way. Hoping I didn't *have* to choose between them. I didn't want to, but I would. It'd be the single most selfish thing I'd ever done in my life, but I'd do it in a heartbeat.

Finally, Ford cracked a smile. "Well then, it's a good thing we all agree with what she said, or this could've been really awkward."

My breath left me in a whoosh, relief rushing over me, though it was short-lived because I hadn't done the hard part yet. I still had to find Luna and get on my knees for her. My family may've been tough nuts to crack, but I hadn't walked away from them without hearing them out. Hadn't asked them to be someone they weren't simply because it fit the narrative.

"Told you that whole opposites attract thing was real," Beck said, looking smug as hell. "You walking over and saying sorry isn't much of a grand gesture, but maybe someone caught what you said on video."

"You're a dick, you know that?" And what the hell did he want me to do anyway? Serenade her while the entire town watched? I didn't have time for that. I needed to do this now, which meant I could only hope that ripping open my chest and showing her my heart would be enough.

Because I needed to find Luna immediately and because I didn't have time for his shit, I threw Beck under the bus. "Why don't you tell everyone else about the romance you're reading this week?"

I slipped away to Ford's, "Like...a dirty one? 'Cause I'd be into that," and didn't look back as I pushed my way through the crowd of people, searching for the only person I needed to see. The only person who could ease this ache in my chest, if only I could prove to her I loved her, just as she was. Not as some diluted version of herself, but as the colorful, vivacious, bright-as-the-sun pain in my ass I couldn't get enough of.

CHAPTER TWENTY-TWO

LUNA

WHILE MY DAD discussed details with Harper and my mom gushed about my homemade creams with a number of the ladies she'd commandeered, I stared at the papers Harper had handed to me, my mouth still hanging open in shock. I'd read the words half a dozen times just to make sure I'd understood them correctly. But yep. No misunderstanding them.

Endangered Species Act.

These papers were this piece of land's golden ticket. Its get out of jail free card. In Harper's research for the maybe-article, she'd stumbled across an environmental impact study that showed not one but *two* endangered species living on this land, which meant it was officially protected. No matter what, Holton Group would never be able to move forward with the build here, and I was hoping, after my speech, the town would push back on any future development possibilities.

The irony of it all was that if that stack of papers had been brought to light earlier, I never would've had to chain myself to that tree, Brady never would've had to take me to the station—twice...for this particular infraction—we never would've struck a deal, and he and I never would've...

Well, we never would've been.

My throat went tight at the thought, the heavy ache of tears stinging my eyes. I hated how we'd left things. Hated even more that I didn't know where he was, where we stood, and that he, apparently, thought I'd had something to do with my parents' arrival and this whole impromptu protest. As if I'd sabotage the resort in that way.

I didn't know what hurt worse—that I'd become less when he'd asked me to, or that I'd done it for a man who believed I'd betray his trust.

Before I could do anything ridiculous like break down sobbing right there in front of half the town, Mabel strolled up, gripped my elbow, and turned me to face her.

"That was an excellent speech, Luna," she said with a grin. "Very moving. Really powerful."

"Thank you." I swallowed down my tears and offered a small smile, fake as it was. "I was flying by the seat of my pants."

"You were doing what you do best." She winked. "I caught it on video. You mind if I post that a couple places?

There's a new app I wanna try. Tock ticks or Ticking Clocks or...some such nonsense?"

I breathed out a laugh. "TikTok, and go for it. I'm not too worried about twenty people seeing it."

She exhaled a relieved sigh, her shoulders relaxing. "Well, honey, I'm glad you said that, 'cause I already posted it. I was just playing the part about not knowing what the app was called—I've been on there for a year. I got sucked into SpicyTok. Some of those books—*whew*." She fanned her face and waggled her brows. "Really spiced up things in the bedroom, if you know what I mean. Anyway, there's a lot more than twelve people who've seen your video."

"What?"

"Oh, you know, just different role-playing games, some light bondage, and—"

"Mabel, no." I held up my hand to stop her. My God, she was as bad as my mother. "What do you mean about the *video*?"

"Oh, right." She turned her phone toward me, showing me the app pulled up on her screen. It was an account titled *StarlightCoveMischief* with only one video posted—of me—and it currently had... Wait. That couldn't be right.

My mouth dropped as I stared at her in shock. "Does this say a hundred and thirteen *thousand* views?"

"You're damn right it does." She shot me a smirk. "Sure beats the handful of people who usually watch my Lives, doesn't it?"

"Holy shit," I breathed, shaking my head. "What does this mean?"

"It means the resort's already getting calls for reservations. Addison's back there, scrambling to take all the forwarded calls. Bookings have gone through the roof." Mabel pursed her lips and tapped a finger against them. "Maybe for the next video, I'll post that one I took of Brady. Where he told his family they could all jump off a cliff for all he cared, as long as he got you."

"He *what*?"

"Jesus Christ, Mabel," a gruff voice I loved said from behind me. And then suddenly, Brady was there. Standing right next to me, his harsh gaze on the older woman. "You don't work for a tabloid. Quit making shit up."

"You didn't say that, Sheriff?" Mabel asked. "Because I heard, and I quote, 'I know you don't agree with Luna, but she's right. Even if she weren't, I'd choose her.' Now, are you trying to tell me I need a hearing aid?"

He didn't even hesitate before he said, "*That* quote you got right."

My mouth dropped open as I stared at him in shock. "You...wait. You told your family that you choose me? What does that mean?"

He turned to me, his eyes boring into mine. "It means I choose you."

"I— But you—" I shook my head, my thoughts as much of a jumble as my words. "What?"

"Can we..." He glanced pointedly at Mabel, then me, before tipping his head to the side.

"Oh, pfft," Mabel said, waving a hand through the air. "You're no fun. I'm gonna see if I can talk Ford into that shirtless interview."

With that, Mabel trotted off while Brady tugged me to the side, tucking us into a cluster of trees away from prying eyes and ears. He ran a hand through his hair, his gaze sweeping over me as if he was reminding himself of my features. As if he hadn't just been inside me an hour before.

"Was that true?" I asked. "What Mabel said."

"The cliff? No. Choosing you? Yes. Always."

I breathed out a humorless laugh and shook my head, unable to believe he'd done that. The man who loved his family above everything else. Who'd chosen them day after day, week after week, year after year, since his mom had died, even above himself. And now, he'd told them he was choosing me...

"That was very sweet, but I'm afraid this is going to be a real kick in the nuts for you." I handed him the papers and watched as he read, his brows inching higher the farther along he got.

When he was finished, he met my gaze. "Okay. What do these mean?"

"It means, all of this?" I swung an arm out to encompass all the commotion around us. "Is a moot point. All my protesting? Completely unnecessary. Redundant, superfluous... Useless. It means you did all that—told your family off and took my side—for nothing."

He stared at me with hard eyes, his jaw clenching as he tossed the papers down on the ground. Then he reached up and cupped my face, brushing his thumbs across my cheeks. "I did it for *everything*. Don't tell me otherwise. I don't care about those papers—I mean, yes, it's great that we have them so we can put an end to this without you chaining yourself to a tree every day and me having to arrest you on trespassing charges courtesy of Holton Group—but I'm *not* sorry I told my family what I did. I meant every single word."

I gripped his forearms as he stared at me, his voice firm and unyielding. This man was so closed off, so isolated, even being the head of his family. Those five pieces of his heart were everything to him, and he'd taken a stand, supported me and my beliefs over them, even when I'd thought he'd abandoned me. I hated that it'd come to that. I didn't ever want to come between them. But I couldn't deny the tiny part inside that grew brighter with his support.

I also couldn't deny that a part of me still ached over what had happened that morning. What he'd asked me to do all those weeks ago. He'd wanted me agreeable, to follow his guidelines. Which I'd done. And then he'd just tossed me aside when things got tough. When a tiny bit of color bled into his black-and-white world. And I didn't want to go through that ever again.

I'd rather go through life with no one than with someone who didn't want the whole me.

"Don't cry, pretty girl." He bent down, kissing away the two tears trailing down my cheeks. "Why're you crying?"

"You hurt me."

He made a gruff sound in his throat, his eyes pained as he stared down at me. "I know I did. I'm—"

"Wait. Please. First, I need you to know I didn't ask my parents to come here. I didn't even know they were planning on it. I can't control what they do—my mom's whims are worse than mine, and my dad only encourages her. And I would've told you that if you'd given me ten seconds of your time this morning before flying off in anger and assuming the worst."

He closed his eyes, rested his forehead against mine, and breathed in deeply. "I know. I fucked up. I was scared and worried about my family, and I didn't stop to think. But I promise, I won't ever do that to you again. I won't ever doubt you."

"You may not doubt me, but will you try to stifle me?"

"What? I don't—"

"The entire basis of our relationship is you trying to shave off the parts of me that didn't allow me to fit into your little box. I don't want that. I *love* me, Brady. I love every part of me, even the ones that aren't perfect. And I can't be me only when it's convenient for you. You either get all of me or none of me."

"I want all of you," he said without hesitation, his voice firm and unyielding.

I reached up and gripped his forearms, my gaze locked with his. "Even the parts that drive you crazy?"

"*All* of you. Especially the parts that drive me crazy. They're the reason I fell in love with you in the first place. I don't want a watered-down version of you. And if I ever try it again, you can tell me to fuck off and find less. I want every bit of you, Luna. Every infuriating, troublemaking, impulsive, unpredictable, out-of-the-box part of you."

My eyes filled until the tears finally spilled over, running down my cheeks as Brady attempted to catch them with his thumbs.

He groaned softly. "Well, I've never told a woman I loved her before, but I'm pretty sure this isn't the desired outcome. I should've gotten Beck's advice on a grand gesture."

I breathed out a laugh, more tears flowing, and shook my head. "No, this is good. This is perfect. This is *you*."

"So, I'm not an ass anymore?"

"No, you're still an ass. But don't worry—I love every frustrating, rule-following, demanding, assy part of you."

His lips twitched, and then a smile spread slowly across his mouth until he was beaming down at me, and sweet fancy Moses riding a bicycle, the sight nearly knocked me on my ass. Probably would've, too, if Brady hadn't tugged my face to his and kissed me.

He held me close, tasting my lips and tongue, and

every time our mouths separated for the briefest of moments, he whispered, "Love you," and I melted into him a little more.

A FEW DAYS LATER, before my parents headed back to Maryland, we had them over for dinner at Brady's house. It was...an experience. Mom spent the entire time sending me not so subtle winks and thumbs up whenever Brady so much as glanced in my direction. She nearly fainted at the table when he pulled my chair out for me, placed a hand on my back, or refilled my wineglass.

Dad and Brady hit it off better than I thought they would, except when Dad got distracted with an email and slipped into work mode while I'd been talking to him. The scowl Brady had sent his way had been potent enough to peel paint. Dad had been oblivious, but I sure as hell hadn't been.

He was always trying to protect me, always looking out for me, even in something as simple as that.

I'd been worried after he'd told me everything at the impromptu protest. Concerned he'd go back on his word or decide that he couldn't handle all of me when it came down to it. But he'd proven every word he said to be true. And I didn't hold back.

He didn't blink when I smoke cleansed him after a particularly rough day dealing with multiple domestic dispute calls. He didn't bat an eye when I promised Mabel and her cronies I would be happy to teach them how to pole dance, if only they found me a studio that had a stripper pole to use. And he'd agreed immediately when I said my parents wanted to have dinner and had only greeted my mother's eccentricities with acceptance.

It was then, after she'd talked about his aura for fifteen minutes straight, that it really sank in. If he could accept my mother at her absolute brightest, not a lumen of her dimmed, then he'd do the same for me.

I glanced up from where I stood at the bathroom vanity, brushing my teeth, to see Brady in the mirror. He leaned one shoulder against the doorjamb, his arms crossed over his bare chest and his eyes on me.

I raised my brows, bending over to spit out the toothpaste before giving my mouth a quick rinse. Standing back up, I turned around to face him. "Am I in trouble, Sheriff?"

"Yes, you are." He pushed off the jamb and took the two steps to me, gripping my hips and setting me on the counter. He slid his hands along the outsides of my thighs, running them up and down along my bare skin. "I just realized I never got my massage or my other yoga class. And since your mom was talking about you going home next week, I figured we better get on that."

"Oh, you just realized, did you?" I bit my lip in an attempt to stop my smile from spreading, but it was no use. Seeing it only made him scowl harder, which, in turn, only made me burst out laughing, though that obviously didn't help the situation.

"I don't know what the hell is so funny," he grumbled, hands frozen on my hips.

"I'm sorry," I said through giggles. "I shouldn't laugh. But you really thought you were being smooth, didn't you?"

"I don't know what you mean."

"No?" I tipped my head to the side as I stared up at him. "So that wasn't you digging for information in a roundabout way rather than just asking me outright if I'm planning on staying?"

His only answer was a tick of his jaw. "So what if it was?"

I rolled my lips in, trying in vain to hide my smile, but it eventually burst free. "I don't plan anything."

"I'm aware," he said with frustration, but his words were laced with nothing but love.

"You know what that means?" I asked, wrapping my arms around his neck and sliding my fingers into his hair.

"What?"

"It means I'm not planning on leaving anytime soon."

He stared down at me, brow furrowed. "I'd prefer ever."

"Don't get greedy. Or bossy. You know I don't like that."

He leaned down, not stopping until our noses brushed. "What I know is you soak my cock when I get bossy with you, so forgive me if I don't believe you."

I gasped. "Rude. And untrue."

Now it was time for him to smile, and it swept over his mouth slow as molasses, the sight of it warming my insides. Then he slid me off the counter and gripped my ass as he walked us into the bedroom. He tossed me on my side of the bed—yes, I had a side, though I spent my nights wrapped around him like a koala—and braced his hands on either side of my head.

"If you needed me to fuck the lies out of you, lawbreaker, you could've just asked. Now, strip."

I could've pushed back, continued on with my little facade—that we both knew wasn't true—or I could strip and have some fun. So, I did what any woman in my shoes would've done when faced with a shirtless Brady, ready to kill her with orgasms. I yanked off my shirt, tossed it aside, and then hooked my leg around his hip, dragging him into me.

"Oh no, Sheriff. What an awful punishment. Next thing I know, you'll be pulling out the cuffs and spanking me."

Brady's answering grin was the last thing I saw before he kissed me. And then he kept kissing me...everywhere, all night long.

EPILOGUE
BRADY

A WEEK LATER, Luna and I drove to the resort for the morning meeting. Her hand was clasped in mine, both of them resting in her lap as she prattled on about a new recipe she wanted to try—not for food, mind you, but for a hair cream—and I was soaking up every word.

After Aiden and Addison had begged and pleaded for her forgiveness surrounding the protest situation—yeah, it was mostly Addison doing the begging and Aiden standing by looking contrite as hell—and then begged and pleaded for Luna to stick around so the resort could provide a well-rounded guest experience, she'd agreed. She'd continued to run her twice-daily yoga classes and was on call to offer in-room massages at a guest's request, which meant she was a permanent—not temporary— resort employee, and thus an attendee of the meetings.

Well, most of them.

Okay, some. And I was pretty sure she was only along for the ride today because Beck had convinced us to have it at the diner instead of the main inn and she was hoping for breakfast. God knew she wouldn't have gotten out of bed otherwise, but food had a way of enticing her.

"So, I'm thinking maybe avocado and mayo." She hummed under her breath, her gaze fixed out the window at the ocean. "That means I'd have to make small batches since they're perishable, but that's okay."

"I'm thinking maybe you're hungry." I pulled up in front of the diner and put the car into park.

She turned to me, a smile tugging up her lips. "I'm starving. *Someone* made me work out this morning before I'd eaten anything."

"I ate plenty."

Head tossed back, she laughed, her eyes sparkling when they met mine. She leaned over the center console until her lips were close enough that I could taste her minty-fresh breath on my tongue. "And I loved every second of it."

Then she kissed me, tentatively sliding her tongue against my bottom lip, but that wasn't nearly enough for me. I dropped her hand and gripped her neck instead, pulling her closer. I might've been inside her not even an hour before, but I couldn't get enough of this woman. Wasn't sure I ever would. If all this equipment weren't in the way, I also wasn't sure I wouldn't have dragged her into my seat, slipped under that flirty little skirt, and tugged her panties aside.

I pulled back, my brows drawn as I glanced down at the wisp of material falling to mid-thigh. "You'd better fucking have panties on under that."

She pulled away with a smirk, then stepped out of the car without answering, her skirt fluttering in the breeze as she went.

I fumbled with the door handle, then my phone and keys, until finally, I clambered out of the car. "Luna, I'm serious."

"Uh-oh... I've activated your scary sheriff voice. I'm really in for it now, aren't I?"

"Lawbreaker, I swear to God, if you're not—"

She cut me off with a laugh, then walked inside the diner as if I wasn't about to lose my shit out here.

I stormed in to find my entire family scattered around the space. Aiden and Addison sat at a table in the center, Beck stood behind the counter with Ford on one of the barstools, and Levi sat at a table in the back, by himself, looking pissed as hell that he had to be here today. And Luna? Luna slid onto a barstool next to Ford and turned to face the rest of the family, smirk in place, her legs crossed and taunting me.

I slid onto the stool next to hers, my jaw tense and shoulders tenser as I tried in vain to see through what she was wearing to find out if she was fucking with me. Logically, I knew she was. Probably. But logic didn't have a place when it came to Luna. I was illogically in love with a woman who enjoyed tormenting me on a daily basis, and I wouldn't want it any other way.

"I think we'd better get you that massage, Sheriff," she whispered in my ear. "You're looking a little...stiff."

Before I could respond, Addison clapped her hands—actually clapped her hands—to get everyone's attention. "Let's get started, shall we? This layout's not ideal, but it will have to do."

"How about those muffins you demolished like they owed you money?" Beck asked dryly. "Were they ideal?"

Ford chuckled. "Mine were delicious, thanks for asking."

"Can we get on with this?" Levi said. "If I have to be here, I'd like it to last as little time as possible."

Addison just rolled her eyes but opened her mouth to speak before an incoming text cut her off. She pulled out her phone, thumbs tapping wildly, as we all sat and waited.

"Jesus Christ, Addison," Levi snapped. "If all the meetings are going to be like this, I'm sending my shit in via email."

"Have a muffin and shut up," Addison grumbled. "It's from Harper."

All eyes landed on Levi, save for Addison's, and I studied him carefully, waiting for a response. The only sign of his irritation, though, was a tick of his jaw. That man was more closed than a book.

"They already approved the article," Aiden said, sipping his coffee. "No take backs."

"She's not taking it back." Addison finally set her phone down and lifted her gaze to everyone. "She just wanted to check and see if bookings were still up thanks to Luna's TikTok debut."

Luna grinned, and I propped my arm on the counter behind us, my hand splayed on her back. I hated that the whole situation had come to that, but I couldn't deny what her being her true self and speaking out had done for the resort, for the family...and for the two of us.

"Which, by the way," Addison continued, "they are. We're officially booked out through June. And in case anyone hasn't been paying attention, that hasn't happened in years."

"Yes, yes, it's very exciting." Beck gestured to the spread. "As you can see, I prepared."

"Oh, you knew this was going to happen, did you?" Addison said.

"Had a feeling, yeah. I also have a feeling Luna's going to want this"—he slid a glass with green toilet water toward her—"and Everly is going to be here in about thirty seconds for her morning pick-me-up." He grabbed a to-go cup and poured coffee into it, then set to fixing it how she liked.

"You're psychic now, huh?" Ford said. "Can I get some of that crystal-ball goodness? Any chances I'll be spending this weekend with some *company*?"

Aiden snorted. "I don't need a crystal ball to tell me the answer to that."

"Yeah, but if—"

The diner door opened, and in walked Everly, who waved to us before taking a seat at a table instead of grabbing the coffee from Beck and heading straight back out like she usually did.

Brows lifted, I asked Beck, "You losing your touch, or what?" Then, to Luna, I said, "Did you actually *want* that disgusting drink, or did he miss the mark on that, too?"

She laughed, elbowing me in the side as she took a large sip. "Mmm...delicious."

Beck rounded the counter, to-go cup in hand, when a man walked in. "Hey, we're not actually open yet."

"Oh, he's with me!" Everly said, before pulling out a menu and placing it on the other side of the table. "We'll just occupy ourselves until you're done."

The guy slid into his seat, his gaze down, his attention never wavering from the phone in his hand. I glanced over at Beck, who was still as a statue, frozen in place, to-go cup in his hand as he stared at Everly and the newcomer. The guy was in his midthirties, with dark, unkempt hair and about three days' worth of stubble. He looked like he'd seen better days, if you asked me, but Beck looked like he was about to have a coronary.

"I don't think his touch is all he's losing," Addison said under her breath, her gaze bouncing back and forth between the couple at the table and Beck, who was maybe three seconds away from having an aneurysm.

"Hey," Levi snapped. "Get your head in the game, man. I'd like to leave as soon as fucking possible."

"Hard agree," I said. "I've got places to be."

With the newcomers to the diner, the rest of us shifted closer, not wanting our business to be broadcast to just anyone who waltzed in. Aiden went through the numbers, and Addison updated everyone on the improvement plans. Meanwhile, Beck's attention kept straying to the table next to the window where Everly and her date sat.

"Your update, Beck?" Addison said.

Beck leaned against the counter, arms crossed as he glared daggers toward the only guests in the diner. His jaw was clenched, face red and only turning redder.

"That's you, man," Ford said with an elbow to his side.

Beck startled, snapping his gaze to us. "What?"

"Quit glowering and fill us in."

"I'm not glowering," he said...with a glower. "I'm just..." He threw his hand out toward the couple. "Do you believe that guy? Everly hasn't stopped talking, and that jackass hasn't looked up from his phone even once."

"And that's a problem for you because..." Addison trailed off, raising her brows as she dared Beck to finish her sentence.

"Because!" he snapped. "She's...she's my friend. And I wouldn't want any of my friends treated like shit. I'd be just as pissed if it were any of you in that situation."

"Uh-huh," Addison said dryly. "I should've figured it'd take another man for you to pull your head out of your ass."

I reached over and slapped Ford on the arm, holding out my hand. "You owe me fifty bucks."

"Dammit," he said, reaching into his pocket to pull out his wallet. "Really thought it was going to be a one-bed situation."

Luna turned to me as I slipped the fifty into my pocket, her brows raised. "What the hell are you two talking about?"

"Romance tropes," Ford said, the duh implied.

"Romance tropes," she repeated slowly.

"Yeah, like, you and Brady were enemies-to-lovers with some heavy opposites attract," he said, his elbow on the counter as he leaned toward her. "But what you've got going right there"—he tipped his head toward Everly and her date and Beck, who glared at them, ignoring every-thing else—"is your classic friends-to-lovers situation where one of the idiots, I mean friends, doesn't figure out they have feelings for the other until they see them with someone else."

"Hmm...interesting."

"Very. Anyone wanna take bets on how long it'll be before Beck kicks him out?" Ford asked our siblings.

I ignored whatever else was said because Luna reached up, running her fingers down my neck and turning my head toward her.

"I was your enemy, huh?" She leaned into me, her eyes sparkling. "That's giving me an awful lot of power."

I gripped her nape and pulled her even closer, brushing my thumb along her neck and reveling in the steady thrum of her heart. A heart she'd given to me. With my lips against hers, I said, "Believe me, lawbreaker, you have a lot more power now as my everything."

OTHER TITLES BY BRIGHTON WALSH

STARLIGHT COVE SERIES

Defiant Heart

————————

HOLIDAYS IN HAVENBROOK SERIES

Main Street Dealmaker

————————

HAVENBROOK SERIES

Second Chance Charmer

Hometown Troublemaker

Pact with a Heartbreaker

Captain Heartbreaker

Small Town Pretender

————————

RELUCTANT HEARTS SERIES

Caged in Winter

Tessa Ever After

Paige in Progress

Our Love Unhinged

————————

ABOUT THE AUTHOR

Award-winning *USA Today* and *Wall Street Journal* bestselling author Brighton Walsh spent a decade as a professional photographer before taking her storytelling in a different direction and reconnecting with her first love—writing. She likes her books how she likes her tea —steamy and satisfying—and adores strong-willed heroines and the protective heroes who fall head over heels for them. Brighton lives in the Midwest with her real life hero of a husband, her two kids—both taller than her—and her dog who thinks she's a queen. Her boy-filled house is the setting for dirty socks galore, frequent dance parties (okay, so it's mostly her, by herself, while her children look on in horror), and more laughter than she thought possible.

www.brightonwalsh.com

 facebook.com/brightonwalshwrites

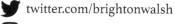 twitter.com/brightonwalsh

instagram.com/brighton_walsh

 tiktok.com/@brightonwalshbooks

Printed in Great Britain
by Amazon

28134270R00157